Enemies Remade

Gwydion Royce

ORACLE OF LOST PATHS BOOKS

Cover Design by Damonza.com

1st edition 2024

Oracle of Lost Paths Books

author@gwydionroyce.com

979-8-9916145-1-1 (eBook)

979-8-9916145-0-4 (Paperback)

CHAPTER ONE

Meg

I wasn't okay. The three men surrounding me stared at me like I'd lost my mind, and maybe I had. Does it seem unhinged to laugh hysterically at impending doom?

"Meg," said Andrus, clasping his hand on my shoulder. "We need to go. Find Felix or Hadi and go."

"We have two days," I said, wiping tears from my eyes. My hands shook as I looked at the smoke that would soon erupt into an explosion that would rain down complete destruction. The pyroclastic flow would bury this city a day after most of Pompeii was wiped off the map.

"Should we travel farther back in time? Even a week?" suggested Gareth.

I was about ready to agree, but then I thought about it. Death had sent us here directly to this time, and I couldn't imagine that he'd just chosen it at random.

"No. It will be easier to search if the city is evacuated," I said.

They gaped at me. "Is that a risk we want to take?" Andrus asked.

"It'll make it quick. Death chose it for a reason."

"Are we sure he's on our side?" asked Remi.

"Did you not see the same thing we did?" asked Gareth. "He knocked Belsioch on his ass."

"That doesn't mean much. He could be posturing. Maybe he wants to take over Belsioch's reign for himself." Remi wasn't giving an inch, and with his stern Roman features, it only added to the severity.

Of course, he had a point. Bel had fooled me enough times for me to realize that. But it made little sense to me. "He's powerful enough to have done that many times over. We'll have to stay vigilant, but for now, let's give him the benefit of the doubt and focus on finding who we're here for."

"Unless they've already caught a boat out of here with the others," said Remi.

I heaved a sigh. "You're going to be the killjoy of the group, aren't you?"

Remi gave me a ghost of a smile. "It brings me great happiness to destroy the hopes of others." He winced and rolled his shoulders, turning away from me as I narrowed my eyes. Personally, I thought Gareth and Andrus had a point about Remi's stubbornness in his refusal of Death's offer to heal him, but I still supported his decision. There was something much deeper to his reasoning that I was determined to get out of him at some point. We'd get to that at the same time we found a moment to address all the other issues our growing family was collecting.

"As much as I'd like to take the time to rest..." I glanced at the volcano smoldering in the not-far-enough distance, then at the sun as it came close to sinking beneath the horizon.

"Let's keep our fingers crossed that on the other side of this one, we can catch a breather," said Andrus.

"From your lips to the Titans' ears," I muttered.

The city streets were full of carts and servants, all heading for the docks. I was salty that we wouldn't have time to explore and made a vow to come back—when annihilation wasn't imminent. We passed one of the luxurious Roman baths and my thoughts wandered to all the trouble my mates and I could get up to in there.

And as often followed thoughts of my mates, the butterflies in my stomach fluttered. This polyamorous relationship would be a lot to figure out on multiple levels. My fear, the one that kept creeping into my mind unbidden, was the worry that we just wouldn't be able to make it work. That we were being drawn together by Fate, and once the mission was over, we would realize that this was a terrible idea. Or maybe they couldn't all get along with each other with me in the middle. Or—and this was my deepest fear—we'd realize our feelings were orchestrated by higher powers with an endgame in mind. And the love wasn't real after all.

Or maybe... I bit my lip, and the painful twisting of my gut and roiling nausea made me lightheaded. What if they realized that their attraction to me was only surface level, and once we didn't have a mission to complete, they'd see me differently?

Would they think I was nothing more than a construct and my value was spent the moment the Titans went free?

No matter what Gareth said, I struggled to believe anyone could fall that fast and hard for me. Yes, I realize I'm digging deep into the angst that plagues teenagers and aging anarchists alike, but it's still a fear. The idea of fates being so deeply entwined is hard to swallow.

Waving away the doubts only works for so long, before they come wandering back. When I'm alone with Gareth, he makes me feel like the only girl in the world. I can wrap myself in that confidence like a fuzzy blanket. But when these men, who have been on this earth far longer than I have—by several millennia—are together... and staring at me... and being their buff, handsome, badass, protective selves... all I can think about is how long it will take before they find out I'm a fraud. Before that pedestal they'd put me on crumbled beneath my feet and I fell into loneliness again.

"—don't you think?"

I blinked and noticed they were looking at me expectantly. "Sorry, what?"

Remi motioned around him at the city that was emptying fast. Most of this district was clear.

"What if he does leave? Or already has?" asked Andrus, worried. "Remi has a point. What if we spend all this time looking for him and he's not here? And we get caught up in the destruction."

"Then we'll have to make our poses interesting for when they dig up our carbonized corpses thousands of years from now." None of the men found my gallows humor amusing. "Okay, give me a minute."

I took a deep breath, regretting it as the ash blanketing everything in a thin film went straight into my lungs. I dragged my clothes over my mouth and nose and tried again.

"Why don't we go in here?" Gareth jerked his thumb toward a large villa, the door already standing open, a trail of treasures spilling into the streets as the owners grabbed what they could and ran.

I nodded. "Good idea."

We hurried in, and Remi shut the door behind us. An ocular skylight filtered in thin light obscured by the dark cloud, leaving an eerie haze. But at least the air was less contaminated.

"I'm going to try and enter a trance. See if I can get a lock on whoever we're here for."

They nodded and fanned out, or at least Gareth and Andrus did. Remi stuck with me. I took a seat on the floor, crossing my legs and closing my eyes. Remi was like a towering presence hanging over me, and I cracked one eye open to find him staring.

"Can I help you with something?"

He shook his head. "Just curious."

"About?"

"How you do what you do," he said, taking a seat next to me.

"Is that all you're curious about?" I asked, unable to hide a lopsided smile.

He shrugged and said nothing, but continued to stare.

"I don't mind if you watch, but could you at least not stare me down? It's kind of distracting."

Remi tilted his head and looked at me askance. I rolled my eyes, and he graced me with a small smile.

Then I closed my eyes and fell. Through a gray abyss, the purgatory between realms. The air currents buoyed me as I caught updrafts and floated before they fell away and I would descend again, until the clouds broke, and I was in a far green country with rolling fields, snowcapped mountains, and lakes as big as oceans. I landed softly on the ground, my fall cushioned by the grass.

But this wasn't just a meditation. I needed to go deeper, and it was a short journey from here. The sun warmed my shoulders, and I tilted my face up to greet it. The deep, verdant green fields muffled my steps, and before me was an enormous tree, an arch cut into the middle. Stepping through it felt like walking through cobwebs, a static that clung to my skin before allowing passage.

The air was several degrees cooler, and I could smell the damp earth as my toes dug into the spongy, loamy soil that was far warmer than the air. As I stepped out into the light on the other side, I was again in an entirely different place.

This sky was in perpetual twilight, a beautiful indigo shot through with silver stars. Two moons hung heavy, casting opalescent light over a landscape of birch, rowan, and oak. Small pools stood in the center of many small clearings that filled the woods. The clearing I was looking for was in the middle of the forest, but it only took a heartbeat to travel there once I set my mind on the destination.

As I stepped through the clearing, a pool of silver glass waited for me. I stared into my reflection, and slow ripples moved in the water. There was no wind. I placed my hand on the surface, barely kissing it with my palm. A hand broke through and wrapped its fingers through mine before pulling me in after it.

The water flowed around me as my doppelgänger dragged me down after it. We stopped and stared at each other before it gave me a calm smile and disappeared. I floated in a liminal space within a liminal space.

I built a mental map of Herculaneum and the city appeared below me. Vesuvius loomed in the distance, a giant threatening wanton destruction. From a vast distance, my mind registered another tremor as the earth shook my physical body. It almost pulled me out of my trance, but a steady hand on my knee eased the worry of being crushed by the falling ceiling. I went back to work.

The map below me shifted, and a path formed. A section of the city to the southeast rose above the others. It was on a slope that a cloud of poison gas, boiling ash, and debris would soon overrun. Grand villas dotted the landscape, three stories high and wide streets of smooth cobbles. A few people darted back and forth, panicked, searching. Their lips moved as they called out names.

But one figure glowed like a beacon, just... waiting. Or maybe not waiting, but... sleeping? There was no doubt this was the Desma, but the lackadaisical reaction surprised me. A volcano was about to destroy the city, and he was napping?

Another more violent tremor and the steady hand gripped me tight. Time to go.

I pushed to the surface of the pool, my head breaching the cool water into the humid air. I pulled myself onto land and returned the way I came without a backward glance. Once I was through the archway in the tree, I traveled up and out of that realm and back into my own, opening my eyes to find three worried faces staring at me.

Andrus blew out a breath. "Good, you're back. We were just starting to debate if we should move you."

I looked at him, confused. The room had become far darker than it had been.

"It was either move her, or hope she's impervious to lava. I think only one of those is a viable option," said Remi.

"I know I shouldn't say it right now, but I can't not," snapped Gareth. "This is one reason it would be *great* to have a guy with bloody *wings* to fly her out of here if needed."

I wasn't sure what was going on, but I knew I wouldn't entertain this argument again. I held my hands out and cut them in a quick motion. "Don't even start. What happened?"

"You'll see in a second, but we should go. Did you find him?" Andrus asked, holding out a hand and helping me to my feet.

"Yes." When Andrus flung the door open, I gasped. The smoke and ash had tripled, massive black clouds belching from the peak. It was going to blow at any minute.

I couldn't see two feet in front of me. I grabbed Andrus's hand and ran toward the place where I'd seen the Desma. On the ground, it was a lot harder to figure distance, but at least I had a mental trail to follow.

I stopped. If I got separated from Gareth or Andrus, I'd be able to find them easily. But Remi was another story. Of course, Andrus knew where my thoughts were going and released my hand, motioning for Remi to come up from the back.

The gargoyle seemed confused but did as he was asked. Without a word, I grabbed his hand and continued to run. When the fear of being burned alive by boiling gasses is very real, it spurs you along with a speed you didn't think you had.

We were closing in on the Desma in good time.

CHAPTER TWO

Meg

My eyes burned as we hurried through the streets. The occasional specter of a terrified person would appear out of the smoke, running in the opposite direction, tears leaving trails through the ash coating their faces. The air was thick and hot, and even with my face tucked into the neckline of my dress, my lungs ached with the poisonous vapors. If we'd been human, even if we made it out of the city, I wouldn't doubt sickness would kill us shortly after.

By the time we arrived at the villa I'd pinpointed in my trance, we were wading through inches of debris, thick like snow. The itch and burn as it singed my skin made me afraid to look at my ankles. I was glad for rapid healing because I couldn't stand to see blisters forming everywhere.

My heartbeat drummed in my ears. Even sound echoed strangely in this gloom, cries from far away warbling and twisting in the heated air, screams from closer by clattering with intensity. A building shattered and its east wall crashed to the ground like a gunshot.

"This is it," I said, stopping in front of a door stained with a russet ochre.

Gareth went through first, checking if the coast was clear. His senses were as muddied as mine in this atmosphere.

Large, arched windows let poison air inside the house so there was no reprieve. The detailed mosaics under our feet had imagery of the trials of Hercules, nymphs and sprites in woodland settings, and the gods on Mount Olympus. The art continued onto the walls, heartbreakingly beautiful frescoes painted with close detail.

"Do you hear that?" asked Remi.

Drunken singing echoed up from deeper in the house.

I coughed and nodded. The noise was drifting up a set of stairs. As we walked down the smooth, worn stairs, the air became cooler and easier to breathe. Torches were lit in their brackets intermittently along the walls, comforting pools of light keeping us company as we went.

The tunnel overhead had begun to collapse, large chunks of stone littering the staircase, the plaster already shattered into spiderweb cracks. The tunnel opened out into a massive hall filled with tables covered in shimmering golden cloth that glowed in the lamplight. Each one was laden with food on fine platters and silver goblets of wine. It was enough to feed an army of hungry nobles, but the hall was quiet and empty.

Except for one man.

"Felix!" Andrus called, hurrying over to the man lying casually on a cushion.

Felix looked around bleary-eyed as we crowded him, unable to focus. A bottle of liquor rolled out of his hand, and he belched.

"Who are you?" he asked. His words were slurred, and he hiccuped before searching for the bottle he dropped. Finding half the remaining contents leaking onto the ground, he grunted and searched for another. "Come to join me for the end?"

He wore gold-embroidered clothes, the lush fabric stifling *me* in this heat. He reeked of sweat and alcohol, and other things I didn't want to think about. His long auburn hair was swept back into a braid, fraying and coming apart after days of not being cared for.

He was tall and lithe, and I could see the faintest points on his ears. Fae, then. His pale skin was smooth and flawless, his features symmetrical and achingly beautiful. But when he smiled, his incisors were long. Dark fae.

We broke eye contact, and he slumped back into his pillows just as another tremor shook the ground. Dishes and cups rattled, and Felix snatched up a full bottle of wine before it toppled over.

The three men formed a shield around me as debris fell from the ceiling and I watched a large crack split across it, like someone was pulling a loose string from a seam.

Felix had lapsed into giggles and was feeding himself grapes that he alternated with bites of a rich-looking mince pie, pouring wine and mead into his mouth straight from the bottle while he was still lying down.

"Come. Help yourselves. All my friends abandoned me when the world started shaking. I'd just had this glorious feast prepared, too."

"This is your house?" I asked.

The only response was a hum of agreement around a mouthful of food and a flippant wave from the hand that appeared over the other side of the table.

"We've come to get you out of here," said Gareth, standing over him with confusion in his eyes.

Felix laughed. "I don't need to be rescued. This is my final stand."

"Against a volcano?" I asked. "That doesn't seem like a fair fight."

He struggled into a sitting position, hanging off the table for support, and tracked my voice with his eyes. I was rewarded with a long, hard stare from slate-gray eyes with blazes of muted green shot through them.

"My final lie down, then," he whispered.

I thought I might've seen recognition somewhere deep in his gaze... but then he belched loudly and crashed back into the cushions.

"Don't you recognize us at all?"

"Should I?" His words were so slurred it was hard to understand him.

When I moved forward, Andrus touched my shoulder.

Andrus leaned in and murmured, "I don't think it's just the alcohol talking."

Instantly, Andrus's problem with Mithras came to mind. "Is he cursed?"

He shook his head. "I think he wanted to forget."

"He blocked us out on purpose?" I looked between the three men, and it was Remi who shed the most light on my question.

"All those years I spent in the dungeons, there were plenty of times where I tried just that. There would be long periods of time where I slipped into... something else. Like there was a blank space in my memory. First, I thought it was something the alchemist was responsible for, but then I realized it was me. Remembering my brothers, the purpose I was supposed to have. It was too painful. And when my memories returned, the pain was even worse. I wanted to sink into that emptiness and put all of you out of mind forever. But I couldn't bring myself to do it. I didn't want to give up the only link I had left to a better time. The memories hurt, but not as much as my everyday suffering."

He jerked his head toward Felix. "But him? Look around. He's living the high life. He has every reason to forget what came before."

Felix spoke from his prone position. "Are you still talking? Come, sit, eat and drink with me. Allow me to be a gracious host before we die."

"Why don't you join your friends on the boats? Escape while you can?" Remi asked, eyes narrowed.

I wasn't sure what he was thinking.

"They were never my friends." He chuckled darkly. "They sure knew how to party though."

"There's still time. You can rebuild your life somewhere else," Remi said.

"Why?" he asked. "I have nothing left if I lose this." Felix motioned around him. "I spent my whole life building this fortune. Vesuvius will destroy it, so I'll let that bitch take me too."

"Your whole life?" demanded Gareth. "Bullshit." He crouched down in front of Felix and tore the bottle from his hand.

"Hey!" Felix tried to grab it back, but Gareth stood. The fae man scowled and reached for another, but Gareth threw it across the room.

Felix stood, the tips of his ears reddening. "I invite you into my house, and this is how you repay me!" He wobbled and barely corrected his balance, playing it off as intentional. "You can give me that back, and leave. I don't need anyone, I'm fine with dying alone."

"Felix," I said, taking a few steps forward. A persistent rumble was sending fine particles of dust from the ceiling. "Don't you feel like you have unfinished business?"

He snorted and seemed to forget the fight he was about to start. "My life has been rich in all things."

"But not companions," I said.

He paused. "I've had plenty of company." He smiled and winked.

I bit back a growl of frustration. "I don't mean conquests, I mean friends. Brothers. A purpose."

"Can't we just drag him out of here?" Gareth asked, looking at us.

"I don't think that's a good idea," said Andrus. "What if it breaks him?"

"How could that cause him damage?" Gareth flexed his arms, ready to throttle Felix and throw him over his shoulder.

"Let's think," said Andrus, snarky. "A bunch of strangers removing him from his delusion and transporting him somewhere else seems like it might be an issue."

Felix looked between them, annoyed, and tumbled back into his nest of pillows. "You should just leave. The last of the boats are gone by now, but maybe you can find something."

There was an idea growing in my mind, but I couldn't quite put it together. There had to be some way I could help. I'd broken Andrus's curse. This wasn't the same thing, but maybe a kick of Titan magick would fix it. I stepped forward and grabbed Felix's wrist. He tried to resist, pulling at me weakly, but he didn't seem to have much strength.

I gathered my magick, channeling it toward my hand and unleashing it, letting it flow through his body. After what I thought was a decent amount of time, because everything at this point was still guess work, I pulled the magick back and released him.

He stared at me, confusion ripe on his face. "What did you just do?"

"I'm trying to help you remember. Do you recognize them now?" I motioned to the men.

Felix turned to them, but nothing changed. "I think you should leave."

I rejoined my mates. "Any more ideas?"

"Can we turn the clock *way* back and try again? We've got the general area that he's in."

I thought about it for a moment. "I don't know. There's no way to tell when he started to lose his memory. Maybe it was before he even got here. We don't have time to keep traveling back to find different versions of him and hope that it's the right one. To be honest, I'm not sure if that would cause trouble. I've always tracked you down in your most current timeline, where you feel you've been living every day like normal. If we took a prior version of him..."

"Time might consider it a paradox and try to fix it," Gareth finished. I could see his wheels turning.

"Yeah," I said, helpless. I hated being at a loss with Time. It was its own being. It had freewill just like everybody else, and it could not be controlled, only partnered with. But just because you knew to expect it didn't make it easier to accept.

"What if—" Gareth broke off, unsure. He was staring off into the distance. Andrus was about to interrupt the wolf's train of thought, but I stopped him with a light touch of his arm.

We waited silently. "What if you overlapped the two versions? Of Felix?"

"I'm listening," I said.

"I keep thinking about how Hermes could jump into a past version of himself, while retaining all of his memories."

Now my own wheels were turning. "Go on."

"Pull a previous version of Felix into this one. Overlap his timelines."

"Not to be the guy that always points out the negative, but that seems like a bad idea," said Remi. "A lot of things could go wrong."

Sometimes I thought the Fates were watching us, like their own personal reality TV show. Every time somebody said something like that, an event would occur that would push us into action, so there was no time to second-guess. An explosion sounded, and we all fell to the floor as the earth shook.

Felix whooped and clapped. "Here she comes!"

Small windows dotted around the room, set high in the ceiling. I hadn't noticed them before in the premature darkness, but now an eerie glow leeched through the gray. A closer look proved my suspicion. We didn't have as much time as I'd thought. Vesuvius had blown her top.

The ash cloud blotted out the sun, turning day into night as the evil glow of molten lava oozed down the side of the mountain. A hellish red light surrounded us, and the heat was just as bad. The first wave of destruction would be hitting Pompeii about now. It might've just been my imagination, but I could've sworn I heard the screams.

"Time's up." I hurried back over to Felix and crouched down.

"Wait wait wait," said Andrus. "Let's just turn back the clock a day, even a few hours. He'll still be in this spot. We can try again when we have a chance to think about it."

I shot him a glance and shook my head, shifting my position next to Felix to get comfortable. "Sometimes logic isn't the best course of action. We do this now."

"But—" he tried again.

"Just give me a minute!" I snapped, regretting it as soon as the words were out. "I'm sorry. I'll explain when we're out of here, but I need space."

All three men nodded and held their ground, looking nervous, but respecting my wishes. I smiled sheepishly. "And maybe back up a few paces? Just in case."

They really didn't look happy about that, but they did it.

I was running through all the possibilities of how to pull this off. My mind kept getting stuck on the last time I'd tried something new, lost control, and sent Gareth into a different realm. I shook it off; I couldn't let myself get distracted by past mistakes. "I am so much stronger now," I whispered to myself.

Felix was shifting uncomfortably, unsure why I was crouched next to him, or why I was staring into him, not at him. I followed his signature down a rabbit hole of time, searching far back, almost to where he would've been dropped off by Kronos.

Felix made to stand, but I gripped tight on his thigh, keeping him in place. He was so startled by my sudden display of strength that he froze.

"Here goes nothing."

I reached out my hand. To my companions, it surely looked like I was grasping thin air, but in my mind's eye I was splitting dimensions. The space around Felix wavered, the air distorting much like it does when I open a portal. But this time, I opened two portals back to back, one in this time, and one in Felix's past. Almost as much to my surprise as to his own, past Felix was there on the other side. He gasped and stared wide eyed at the strange scene that must've appeared before him. I pushed past the resistance of the barriers, reaching for him.

He was reluctant to take it, but I looked at him calmly, my hand never wavering. Current Felix squirmed harder to get away now that he saw this doppelgänger of himself, horrified.

"Please," I said. "I will give you all the answers I can, but please trust me. I am Kronos's daughter." A strange feeling went through me as I said those words, after the grudges I'd held for so long. And yet I knew it for truth.

Past Felix stared at me, and slowly, his posture relaxed. Whatever sense it was that allowed the others to know me on sight must've been working for him because at last he nodded and took my hand. I gripped it tight and pulled. There was a strong resistance between the portals, but past Felix emerged into the present, took a moment to consider the fresh hell he'd just stepped into and then both bodies merged, overlaying on top of each other.

Felix's whole body shuddered and went limp. "Shit," I hissed, putting my ear to his chest. I could still hear his heart beating, and he was breathing.

He chuckled with a deep, rumbling sound, and I sat back on my heels.

"That's a neat trick," he said, sitting up and stretching. "What the hell am I wearing? Gold embroidery? Why is it so hot in here?"

The other three men all breathed sighs of relief, which caught Felix's attention. He jumped to his feet and bounded over to his friends. There was laughter and back slapping all around until I cleared my throat.

"I hate to bust up this reunion, but Vesuvius is about to turn this place into our tomb."

They all turned back to face me, and Felix looked at me with fresh eyes. "Megiste."

I held up my hand, moving to rejoin them. "Meg, please. But we need to go."

Gareth gave me a kiss before Andrus wrapped me in his arms. Remi stood there with his usual stoic detachedness.

I grinned as I decided on our destination. Hadi was the only one left to find, but with Remi still coming to grips with... everything, and Felix having been a guinea pig for a new magick I'd just pulled out of my ass, we needed to regroup. We could figure out what to do about the Hounds when we landed. And boy, was this place going to be a shock to their systems.

I tapped into the time stream, and we were off.

CHAPTER THREE

Andrus

I was drowning in noise. We snapped back into time in the middle of a crowded city street, a group of men with brass instruments dancing their way down the avenue with a huge gathering of celebrants in their wake. A man with long sticks for legs, at least nine feet tall, in a bright purple, green, and gold suit almost tripped over us and stepped into the path of a metal and glass cart laden with food pushing through the tight crush of people. The cart veered in our direction and Remi grabbed Meg, pulling her out of the way and shielding her with his body as the man and cart rattled off, casting us an odd glance as the crowd swallowed him.

"Are you alright?" Remi asked in French, looking her over as she gave him an amused grin. It looked like she was breaking through the gargoyle's barriers.

"I'm fine," she said, also in French.

"What is this place?" yelled Felix in Latin, hands clamped over his ears. Compared to a city, mid-ravage, at the whims of a volcano, I didn't think it was much different. As I looked around me, this chaos slowly began to make sense. Words came, labels for the things I was seeing, and their purpose.

"Hey! Toga, toga—" chanted a man, looking at us as he sloshed a large amount of brightly colored liquid from an oddly shaped cup as he raised it in the air. Alcohol, and powerful stuff at that. As I picked out individual conversations, I could tell most of them were speaking... modern English. American English.

Meg grabbed Felix's tunic and pulled him after her down an alley. We all followed as she ducked through the narrow walk, lit by small glowing lights that twinkled overhead. Electric bulbs. Excitement stirred within me. Instant light.

She seemed to know where she was going, and the noise tapered a little as we moved until we could at least hear each other speak.

We ended up in a small courtyard. Gareth was spinning in slow circles, taking in the scenery. He was less alarmed by this place than Felix and Remi as he studied it, perhaps with Time whispering in his ear. He was figuring out what he was looking at, but in a different way than I was.

A call from a balcony overhead caught our attention, and a woman with large breasts pulled up her shirt and screamed drunkenly.

"Sorry," Meg called back. "No beads."

"That's okay, just send those fellas up here," she said, tripping and falling into her friend, who looked annoyed. The sober one waved at us and pulled her friend through a pair of ornamental doors. Sheer, gauzy curtains were blowing in the breeze, and something made from large, flat blades was spinning from the ceiling. A fan.

More of those twinkling lights were all around us, and a fountain in the middle of the space gurgled. There were more small groups here, giving us a lot of attention. I couldn't blame them. We must've looked a mess, covered in ash and blood and gods knew what else. Several women fixed us with lusty gazes as the men they were with eyed us with immediate dislike.

"Excuse me." A woman had stopped and was looking at us with a mixture of concern and keen interest. "Do you need help? You don't seem like you're happy to be here." She peered closer and backed away in alarm. "Is that blood?"

Meg stepped forward. "Sorry, no. We're fine. We're filming a movie down the street and we got separated from our group." Meg rolled her eyes and gave a small laugh. "This is the last time I let them convince me to leave the set in costume, you know?"

"A movie? What one?" The woman's eyes roved over us, lit up with pure desire now that she didn't need to worry about summoning help.

"Can't say, the studio would be pissed. We really need to get back to set."

Meg pulled us along once again until we turned the corner out of sight onto a street that was far less crowded. I could still hear the revelry from the street we'd appeared on and watched inebriated people stumble by on their way to the next round of debauchery.

Something snapped Felix out of his wordless trance. Still in Latin, his mouth forming the unfamiliar word with discomfort, he asked, "What's a movie?"

I smiled, remembering when I'd first heard the word. Meg's excitement when she spoke of things from her life before all this that gave her joy was contagious.

She grinned. "It's like when a bard tells a story and people act it out."

Felix hummed thoughtfully and looked around him, less tense now that the noise wasn't so overwhelming. "Whose territory is this?"

It took Meg a second to figure out what he was asking. "The United States. It's a country."

More questions were forming as Felix went down the inevitable rabbit hole, but we didn't have time. Meg wouldn't cut him off, but I had no such qualms.

"There will plenty of time for questions, but I'm sure Meg has a plan in mind for where we're going. Is Hadi here?" It didn't seem right, since we were all sent backward, but I wouldn't put anything beyond the realm of impossibility.

She shook her head. "No. I brought us here because it will give us a good place to hide. Nobody will look twice at a bunch of weirdos in 1980s New Orleans, during Mardi Gras no less. And this city has plenty of Strangers everywhere, so we'll fit right in."

"Do you think the Hounds will still come for us? Won't they go after Hadi?" asked Remi.

She nodded. "At least until they figure out that Death is gone."

"Is there some way we can expedite that? What if they bring Hadi back there and kill him in retaliation?" asked Remi.

"Or will they turn on Belsioch?" I asked.

Gareth spoke up. "I would imagine it would be the latter. Unless Belsioch trades them for something else even bigger."

That idea hung in the air between us all. Was there such a thing to offer? I shuddered at the possibilities.

"Let's hold onto the thought that they'll be out of the pic-ture for now. Maybe I can find a way to send them a message."

"And draw their attention to us?" Remi looked incredu-lous.

"It's not ideal, but we are in no position to go hunting for him. We need to get our feet under us before we go after him. Otherwise we're a group of disorganized schmucks that are just as likely to get ourselves killed as find Hadi. We need to build an offensive. I'm tired of running."

"Small comfort if he dies because of our delay," said Remi.

Gareth and I turned on him, furious, but Meg stopped us. "Death said he would help if they do show," said Meg, a sudden chill making her shiver. Being the closest, I pulled her to me and wrapped my arms around her.

"If we sent up a flare," said Remi. "Hadi wouldn't know to do that."

Gareth had violence written all over his face. "This is what she's talking about, asshole. Until we can function as a team, we have no business going forward."

An uneasy silence fell between us until a second line passed the intersection up the street, the brass band leading a parade of dozens of revelers.

"So where do we go?" I asked, kissing the top of her head.

"I have a friend who lives nearby. She's a sphinx, so be on your best behavior."

Gareth choked in surprise. "A sphinx?" He slapped his chest. "How'd you end up making *friends* with one of those?"

Meg shot him a glare. "That's what I'm talking about. She'll rip you to pieces if you show her any disrespect."

"Aye," said Gareth. "I'm aware." He cast a pointed glance at Felix and Remi, and I did the same.

Felix, for his part, looked indignant. "What? I can behave."

Remi rolled his eyes, switching seamlessly to Greek like he'd never stopped speaking it. "Right. It was a huge stretch for you to lose yourself in the hedonism we found you in."

Meg and Felix spoke in unison. "When in Rome."

She burst out laughing, and we stared at her. "Is this another joke we'll understand at some point?" I asked. The lexicon rarely covered subtext.

This only made her laugh harder. "I didn't even think about that!" She turned to Felix, tears streaming down her face over pink cheeks. "You were being literal! When in Rome!" She was sagging in my arms, in hysterics.

Once she caught her breath and wiped tears from her eyes, she explained. I guess I could see the humor, but the funnier part was Remi's stoic grimace.

If she could eek a genuine smile out of him some day, I'd be shocked. I don't think I've ever seen one.

"Let's get to this sphinx, then," said Felix, now in Greek. "So I can prove to you all that I'm an upstanding gentleman."

"She lives in an amazing house, but I'm warning you. It's incredibly haunted. I'm not sure if either of you gained my mediumship ability—" She glanced between Gareth and I. "—but this will be a great place to find out." The mischievous look in her eye made me nervous.

We walked several more streets up, the quiet pierced only by crickets. This neighborhood was old, wisteria and Spanish moss making eerie shadows with the light of the gas lamps. She finally stopped in front of a large estate, fenced off with a small yard and *No Trespassing* signs. But the wards around this place would drive anyone away.

The house itself was three stories, with massive columns in the front. Every window had heavy wooden shutters and the ones on the bottom floor had intricate ironwork securing them. Meg rang a bell hanging from a post by the gate and we waited.

After several minutes, during which Felix fidgeted nervously, the door creaked open, and a regal woman appeared.

She was tall and thin, with wide shoulders and long black hair that fell in thick curls to her waist. Her smooth brown skin contrasted with her true age, which hid behind her keen eyes. She might've been as old as us, maybe even older. Her hands were clasped easily in front of her and she walked with a graceful, catlike gait.

As she reached the fence, her eyes flashed briefly, bright green with slit pupils, before they settled back into their human shape.

"Megiste," she said, her warm timbre causing the hairs on my neck to rise. "And guests." She smiled, the cupid's bow of her bright red mouth lifting to reveal pointed teeth. "You honor me with a visit." She undid the clasp on the gate and swung it open. "I am Farah. Please, come in."

We looked at Meg uncertainly. Sphinxes rarely allowed entry without a game of riddles. It was encoded into their very beings.

Meg gave us pointed glances and stepped confidently forward, so we followed.

Once we were inside the house, all I could do was stare around me in amazement. There were treasures from all over the world, from places that had already ceased to exist by the time I was born.

"Amazing, isn't it?" Farah asked, and I jumped, not realizing she'd moved directly behind me.

"Yes," I said. "You have a lovely home."

She smiled coquettishly and turned to Meg. "You'll be staying for a little while?"

Meg nodded. "If it's not too much trouble." Just behind my mate, I could see the hazy outline of a person just standing there, and I huffed. Ghosts.

"I have a large suite on the top floor, but I'm not sure the bed is big enough for all of you," said Farah with a smirk.

Meg blushed. "That's perfectly fine."

The sphinx appraised us again. "Oh. You're only mated to two of them?" She turned to Felix and Remi. "What did you two do wrong?"

Remi scowled, but Meg jumped in with an answer before the surly brute could get us in trouble. "Things have been very hectic."

"Ah. Well." She clasped her hands again. "I'll make sure everything you need is taken care of so you'll have plenty of time to get to know each other."

Meg palmed her face, her color deepening. "Farah, come on." Her tone was pleading.

The sphinx laughed, a sparkle in her eye. "I think your embarrassment is adorable. I'm sure these gentlemen agree."

Farah reached for a hand bell sitting on a side table, the sound summoning a housemaid. "If you could show our guests to the third floor? Thank you, Pauline."

Our group followed Pauline dutifully, and Meg gave Farah a grateful nod as she passed. My tension eased at Meg's relief. The worry-lines around her eyes that had been a constant for the last week made way for a smile. As Meg got within a foot of Farah, something changed.

The sphinx's hand shot out and grabbed her wrist. "Wait."

Gareth whirled, eyes flashing yellow. My teeth extended in a snarl.

Meg waved us both off with a warning glare.

Farah leaned in close, nostrils flaring as she inhaled Meg's scent. "Do you want to explain to me why you smell like the Hounds?"

Meg's shock was plain. "How—"

"Tell me!" she snapped.

Our mate blanched, worried but not fearful. There must be a hell of a story behind their friendship for her have no fear of this creature.

Farah stared until Meg relented. "We had a run-in. Bel hired them when he couldn't kill us himself." She sighed, the anxious eye-creases returning. "We won't be staying long. We just needed a safe place to rest."

Our host's posture eased, and she released Meg. "Nonsense. You can stay as long as you need. You're about ready to drop from exhaustion."

Meg shook her head. "They're on the trail of Hadi already. We're just here to recuperate for a bit, maybe a day, but that's the most we can risk. If they find him before we do—"

"What will they do with him when they find him?" asked Farah. Her irises were gleaming, lines of gold swirling through the green as she stared into Meg.

"Take him to Bel. But since Bel was supposed to capture Death for them as their payment, and Death is no longer there for them to collect... I don't know what will happen. And I don't want to find out. As soon as we're rested up enough—" Meg paused and gave a hard look at Remi. "—and hopefully working as a team, we'll be out of your hair."

Her eyes drifted in thought. In a soft voice, Farah said, "So Bel's bargain with them is void. They just need to learn of this before they find your other mate."

Meg nodded. "I was thinking about passing them a message, but as Remi pointed out, it might bring them to us."

Farah went silent for a long moment. "Let me see what I can do."

"No. I can't ask you to do that." Meg's sudden frantic worry for her friend had me wrapping my arms around her. "I can't let you put yourself in that kind of danger on my behalf."

"I wouldn't be in danger. Not any more than usual." The golden glow in her eyes vanished as she seemed to make up her mind. Before Meg could ask the question clearly on her lips, Farah continued. "There are many things you don't know about me, child. Including the circles I run in." She gave us all a determined smile. "Just leave this to me."

"Farah—"

"It's not open for discussion. Now go."

Meg hesitated still.

"I will give you an update in the morning."

End of discussion.

Pauline inclined her head and led the way up two narrow sets of stairs, each hallway we passed through lined with more shelves of treasures. Almost every inch of wall space was covered in art. On the second floor, a glance through a set of double doors at the end of the hall made me pause.

A library, full to bursting with shelves laden with leather-bound books. I took a step closer to sneak a peek inside, but Pauline moved past me and closed the doors.

"That's the mistress's personal library. You'll need her permission to enter." Her tone clearly implied what would happen if I didn't have it.

I smiled and nodded. "Of course."

She led on to a spiral staircase that landed us on the third floor. The attic was a wide-open living space of plush furniture, a fireplace, and large windows overlooking a swamp. Pauline pointed down a short hallway.

"Those doors at the end are for the suite. The other doors on either side are for smaller guest rooms, should you need 'em." She eyed us with mild curiosity, but when we had no questions, she shrugged. "Melvin will be up with food for y'all shortly. There should be extra clothing in the dressers, you can help yourselves." She frowned as she looked at Gareth and Remi. "Not sure they'll fit you though."

Felix snickered, and Pauline looked abashed. "I'm sorry, I didn't mean—"

"Not at all," said Meg, smiling. "That's a very generous offer, thank you."

Pauline nodded and left.

Meg sat heavily on the couch, and we surrounded her.

Gareth slung his arm around her shoulder. "Farah seems more than confident that she can do this. Dropping word with the Hounds should be all it takes. No direct contact."

"It's still so risky," said Meg, shaking her head. "What if—"

"No," said Remi, crouching in front of her.

"No?" asked Gareth, eyebrow dangerously peaked.

"Stop worrying," Remi continued, ignoring the wolf. "Your only job is to get your mind focused. You need to let Farah do whatever she's planning. If it doesn't work, she'll tell us in the morning, and we'll go from there."

Meg gave a small smile and eventually nodded, grasping Remi's face in her hands. "Thank you." When she removed her hands, she rubbed her fingers together, realizing how grimy we all were.

"Okay, we can deal with that." Meg looked at us. "Who's first?"

CHAPTER FOUR

Gareth

Remi's mouth dropped open, Felix started drooling, and Andrus blinked rapidly as we took in Meg's words.

She looked between us, confused at the reactions, before turning a shade of red so deep I could feel the heat radiating from her. "Oh, my—that's not what I meant!"

I laughed and she jabbed me with her elbow, trying to hide a begrudging smile. "I meant, I think we're all in need of a bath—"

Andrus cocked his head and my grin grew wider.

"—separately!" she quickly added. "There's only one bathroom up here. I'm sure we could use the others, if we asked." She gestured down the stairs. "I'm still wet—" She slapped a hand over her mouth as my grin turned predatory. "Dammit!" She stomped her foot, laughing at herself.

"I mean, I was soaked through—" Her mouth snapped shut and she took a breath. Felix and Andrus were laughing outright, and my shoulders were shaking as I attempted to hold back my laughter. Her discomfort was cute. None of us were interested in putting her out of her misery. Remi was staring at her curiously, not quite smiling, but not with his usual moroseness, either.

She tried one more time. "My *clothes* were soaked through with sweat and volcano dust, and they're still a little damp."

"Right." I shrugged. "I knew that's what you were saying the whole time." A new round of laughter went up and Meg tried to tackle me, but I swept her up and threw her over my shoulder.

"Let's find that—what did you call it?—bathroom, shall we?"

"Count me in," said Andrus, following.

"Wait," said Meg.

She addressed Remi and Felix. I heard the shy hesitancy in her voice. "If you'd like to, um, join us... you're welcome to."

Felix didn't hesitate. No surprise there. But when I didn't hear Remi, I turned. Meg slapped my ass. "Either put me down or turn around." So I split the difference, angling so we could both look over at him.

Remi shook his head. "I don't think that's a good idea just yet." Without another word, he walked down the stairs and disappeared.

"What's his problem?" asked Felix.

I sighed. "There'll be plenty of time to talk later. Right now, there's only one thing we need to focus on." My hand settled on the rounded globe of my mate's ass and my cock was already rising, imagining all the sounds she'd make with the three of us pleasing her.

"Second door on the right," said Meg. Andrus opened it and we followed.

Time had been helping me figure things out, feeding me a constant stream of information about the modern world. Granted, it was from the viewpoint of a consciousness older than the universe itself, so small things, like the setup I was looking at now, didn't really make sense. At least Felix was having the same issues.

Gleaming metal and glass were everywhere. I set Meg down and she moved to a large cube made of glass, opened a door, and stepped inside. She peeled off her ruined clothes and tossed them out before turning knobs on the wall and standing aside as a torrent of water cascaded from a golden disc suspended from the ceiling.

I caught sight of Felix as he drank in the sight of her. I remembered the first time I'd laid eyes on her. Overwhelming lust, the drive, the need to consume her. To make her mine. But as that pure desire abated, deeper feelings took over. I know Andrus's experience was similar, and I've seen the way Remi looks at her when he thinks nobody's watching. His issues aside, there's no denying how he craves her.

Now Felix was at the start of that same journey. Wanting her out of primal attraction. I'd seen Felix use women and discard them like they were nothing, and my alpha instincts roared to the forefront. I wouldn't allow *anyone* to disrespect my mate and use her like that. He may be a brother to me, but I'd watch him closely, nonetheless.

Meg adjusted the knobs until the water steamed. "Are you going to join me, or just stand there?" she teased.

It was clear from the experience with Andrus that all the mates needed to be involved before the bonding could work. I wasn't sure if there was a specific order to be adhered to, but I couldn't hold myself back from her.

I stalked forward, marveling only for a moment at the hot water streaming over us before I claimed her lips with my own. Andrus moved behind her, pulling her wet hair from her neck and running his teeth over her throat as he pressed against her.

She was melded between us, grinding against my hardening cock. Andrus groaned, and she mewled as his fingers found the already stiff pink buds of her nipples. She pressed harder into me, and a growl rumbled from my chest. I needed her so badly, my hands finding her hips and gripping her smooth skin as I devoured her with a kiss.

As we came up for air, I saw Felix observing us. I respected his restraint. Letting his soon-to-be mate get comfortable with us before he joined the play. He unbraided his hair with a feral intensity in his gaze.

"We should get clean before we get dirty," she said with a sideways grin, breathless and flushed, the color in her cheeks making her so irresistible it took all I had not to press her against the wall and bury my cock inside her.

She slipped out from between us, and we watched her intently as she retrieved the soap, building a lather and running her hands down Andrus's body. He stood still, watching as she took her time rubbing him down, casting sidelong glances at me and Felix. She moved on to me, washing each ridge of muscle and intricate tattoo before kneeling back in front of Andrus.

She slicked her hands over his thighs while the water cascaded over them, rinsing the soap away. Her lips parted, tongue running over her top lip, and I watched with hooded eyes as she swallowed his cock, her hands gripping his ass. His head tilted back with a placid smile as his fingers twined in her hair. She reached for me and stroked as she bobbed faster, moaning around his cock as he drove his hips forward until Andrus thrust his completion with a groan.

When he was spent, she stood, still stroking me. She knew I needed to feel her tight walls around me, turning and stretching to wrap her arms around my neck as I entered her from behind. A shuddering sigh tumbled past her lips as I pushed into her slick channel, the muscles convulsing as her pussy gripped me.

I thrust, the sound of her moan echoing in the small space just as wonderful as I thought it would be. I continued as Felix stepped forward, taking the discarded soap and building a lather before he explored her body, studying every curve as he washed her, the water cascading over us as we stood right in the center.

Her body tightened and I picked up my speed, running my tongue over the mark I'd left on her shoulder. Her pussy clenched around me, and she cried out, moments from climax. Felix sucked her nipple into his mouth and she came, her ecstasy rolling through me and bringing me to the finish.

With one last thrust, I emptied myself into her. I bit down on her shoulder. I didn't break the skin, but her nails raked the back of my neck and pulled at my hair as her cries redoubled. It took a full minute for her to come down. I wrapped my arms around her waist as she let go, supporting her trembling knees. I took a smug satisfaction in that.

I eased out of her and lifted her in my arms, exiting the shower and making sure her feet were steady on the plush rug before grabbing a towel. With a light brush across her breasts, I moved it lower. She bit her lip, but Meg stopped me and took the towel from my hands. "Let's not get carried away," she laughed.

I chuckled and retrieved another. Andrus did the same as Felix washed himself thoroughly, struggling with knots in his hair. He always took great pride in his appearance and for it to have become so unkempt spoke volumes about how he'd been living. I'm sure it wasn't easy coming to grips with the oblivion he'd sunk into, the hopelessness that had consumed him as he drowned it in drink and debauchery.

"Join us when you're ready," I said, not wanting to rush him. "We'll take our time getting to the fun."

He nodded at me, relief flashing across his face. Maybe it hadn't been restraint after all, but nerves that kept him from jumping in at first. We'd all suffered in our own ways, these long years of waiting.

The three of us made our way to the bedroom. Farah wasn't kidding. The bed was large enough for three of us to sleep easily, and during play, nobody would have to be left out.

We peeled the ridiculous, thick bedspread back and Andrus and I took up positions on either side of our mate. We whiled away the time, stroking, caressing and kissing, tender words passing between the three of us as we waited for Felix.

Ten minutes later he appeared, the confidence of the man I remembered having returned in full. Meg held her hand out to him and he stepped forward. I moved, standing off to the side as Felix took my place next to her, taking her face in his hands and kissing her with the same longing and passion I remember feeling my first time with her.

He moved down her body, lavishing attention on her breasts before kissing down her stomach and moving between her thighs. He gripped her knees and pushed them apart, his fingers parting her folds before delving into her entrance. Her back arched, and he continued to pump his fingers as he lowered his head and licked her, centering his tongue on her nub. She gasped, her hands twisting in the sheets.

Andrus watched until he couldn't hold himself back any-more. He leaned over, capturing her next moan as he closed his mouth over hers. His hand trailed to her breast, and he cupped it before twisting his fingers around her nipple.

Felix continued, and I prowled around the bed, watching her intently as she writhed underneath them. Felix pushed his fingers deeper and she broke away from Andrus to scream her release. He continued to lick her and when he finally raised his head, his eyes were solid black.

Meg reached out to me and Felix moved aside. She was ready to start the bonding.

She moved onto all fours near the edge of the bed and glanced at me over her shoulder. I ran my hands over the globes of her ass before dipping my fingers into her pussy, working one digit past the tight ring of her back entrance. She dropped her head and let out a low moan, slowly working herself back and forth on my finger. I added another, and she repeated the process.

"Take me," she breathed.

I moved behind her, easing into her passage as she pushed back into me. By the time I was fully sheathed, we were both breathless. I pumped into her, starting with small strokes. She added backward thrusts of her own and I spurred my pace as magick flared to life.

It swirled around us, much stronger than the first two bondings. Both of us cried out as overwhelming sensation took us, every nerve ending singing with pleasure as our bodies be-came a single soul. Our breathing synced and our heartbeats matched pace as they thrummed in our chests.

Felix gasped. Meg's eyes must be shining with their rainbow of colors. We crashed together and she held her hand out for

Andrus. A sudden flash of thought showed me with detail what Meg had in mind.

"Aren't you getting creative?" I asked, fisting my hand in her hair and raising her to her knees, enjoying a few deep, languid strokes that coaxed a high-pitched cry from her. Meg grasped both hands between her thighs before running them up her body and cupping her breasts.

Andrus kneeled in front of her, nudging her thighs wide and situating himself between them as she grasped his cock. I paused my movements as she lined up and sank down. A waft of lavender perfume washed over me as her silver hair cascaded down her back, her head tilting back to expose her neck. I grasped her throat, caressing the smooth skin. My grip tightened ever so slightly, her approval thrumming through the bond.

She rode Andrus and I matched the rhythm, alternating my strokes with his. The red ring gleamed around the outer edge of the rainbow of her eyes, and I was struck dumb by her beauty. A goddess in our midst.

She gripped Andrus's shoulders, her fingers transforming into claws. When a howl worked its way from her throat, I moaned, overcome. I spurred our pace faster, knowing I couldn't keep this up for much longer.

Meg took one of my hands from her hip and raised it to her lips, running them along my wrist before her hot tongue teased me, asking permission.

"Yes," I groaned, thrusts sporadic and rough. "Do it."

Her fangs sank into me, and she drank. My control fell utterly away. I came with such force I almost sank to my knees, and when she released my wrist I stumbled back, spent. I'd never been fed on before, but I was already looking forward to the next.

Andrus gripped her ass, raising her higher so he could thrust into her with abandon. They stared at each other as they lost themselves to the pleasure until Andrus pulled her close and sank his teeth into her neck.

Still connected, I felt every bit of their ecstasy as they both shattered, crashing together as they came. Felix moved next to Meg, kissing her as Andrus wound down. Her tongue tangled with the dark elf's as she rode out the last shudders of her orgasm.

Andrus helped shift Meg off him, just the faintest smudge of blood on his lips. Felix joined her on the bed, and she pushed his shoulders until he was lying back flat. He held her face in his hands, staring into her incredible eyes with wonder etched onto his face. She kissed him before rising up and positioning herself over him, teasing his tip through her folds.

He groaned as she sank down, taking all of him in one movement. She rode, the pace agonizingly slow as she caressed his chest. And then... she glowed.

An ethereal light surrounded her, growing brighter as the tips of her ears molded into perfect points. The bond locked into place between them, the tension snapping taut with a crack. Felix cried out as the magick overtook him, bucking against her. He rose, switching their positions and settling between her thighs before setting a grueling pace, ravaging her as she writhed beneath him, her claws raking against his skin gently enough to leave no trace.

Her knees clamped tight over his hips as she rocked with his thrusts. I was hard again and I stroked myself off, the crescendo of her moans almost making me come as I watched them.

Then the magick completed its circuit between us. Andrus and I gasped as Felix joined the single entity that the bond made of us.

Andrus was standing nearer the two. Completing the bond had his cock rising to attention. Without even looking, Meg reached out, stroking his length. She and Felix came together and the shared sensation sent Andrus and me to finish with them.

Felix collapsed on top of her as they caught their breaths, stealing small kisses as they waited for the aftershocks to subside.

We piled around Meg in bed and she rested her head on my chest with a contented sigh. She peered up at me. "Do you think they brought food up yet?"

Chapter Five

Remi

The entire household could hear what was happening upstairs. I came out of the bathroom—having been shown by a gracious butler how to use the *shower,* he called it—with a towel wrapped around my waist and feeling more normal than I had in years. A man with a trolley laden with food hesitated at the foot of the stairs.

Then the sounds of Meg and the others made it to my ears, along with the potent vortex of magick swirling in the air. I tapped the man on the shoulder and through a series of pantomimes, I told him I'd bring the meal up myself.

A couple of trips and the table in the common area was full of dishes and a quick search of the wardrobes revealed ill-fitting but passable clothing.

Things in the bedroom had quieted down and I was enjoying a meal while exploring my surroundings. I made the mistake of flipping something on a large metal box and sound blasted out of it as lights flickered over its face. Panicked, I began turning and flipping anything that moved, unable to remember which one I'd hit initially.

When everything fell silent again, I heard a soft snickering behind me. Meg was standing there, wrapped in a sheet, looking like an exhausted angel as a glow emanated from her.

"*Mes dieux*," I whispered.

"That bad?" she asked, trying and failing to remove stray hair from her face.

I crossed the room and tucked the strands behind her ear, my fingertips grazing her now pointed ears. "No, not bad. Breathtaking." I studied the aura surrounding her more closely. "You are glowing."

"Really?" she asked, putting a hand to her cheek. She stepped to a full-length mirror on the wall. "What caused that?"

"I did," said Felix from the hallway. "Naturally." He puffed out his chest and circled his arms around Meg's waist.

"Or it could be his power of illusion settling in with the rest of your abilities," said Andrus, walking into the room. He kissed Meg on the top of her head as he passed before he spotted the food. "Fantastic. I'm famished."

"Could be. But I think my theory is better," insisted Felix, giving Meg one more squeeze before joining Andrus at the table. Down the hall, I heard the bathroom door close.

They had both found pants like the ones I was wearing, made of a thick, warm material with drawstring closures. I didn't know what they were called, but they were far more comfortable than the wool trews I was used to. Before the dungeons alleviated my need for clothing entirely.

Had it only been a few days since I was trapped there, waiting for the end? That cold dark closed around me, the chill stealing into my bones. With that cursed stone limiting my healing ability, it's a wonder I didn't succumb to the combination of filth, sickness, open wounds, and the constant bitter damp.

"Remi? Are you okay?" asked Meg, touching my shoulder.

I startled and looked around at her. "I'm fine."

She grasped my hand. I'd reached for the lump of scar tissue left behind when the Hound ripped the stone from my flesh.

"Are you sure?" She looked into my eyes with such earnest tenderness, it took my breath away. How could she look at me like that? I'd treated her horribly, was pushing her away every chance I had. My refusal to allow the restoration of my wings was reckless. And I'd been furious when they refused to leave me behind. I didn't deserve that kind of compassion.

"Yes, I'm sure." I pointed at the metal box with its cursed levers. "I'm still recovering from my run-in with that thing."

"A stereo," said Meg. "It plays music."

"Is that what that was?" I asked, genuinely curious.

She laughed, a clear, joyous sound. Her bonding had enlivened her to a level I hadn't yet seen from her. It was intoxicating, contagious even.

"Trust me. I'll put together a music selection of modern classics that will blow your mind," she reached over and snapped up some cut fruit from the table, taking a bite of fresh peach. I watched a dribble of juice drip down her chin and licked my lips.

"Gods, man, just admit it."

I blinked and looked at Andrus. "What?"

"You don't want out of your oaths to the Titans. You're being a curmudgeon." He grinned. "But you do want to join in the bond."

Meg blew out a breath. "But we'll have to table that for now, because I don't think I can take any more tonight. I need electrolytes and a good night's sleep." She finished the fruit, grabbed a slice of bread thick with butter, and devoured it. "I'm going to go clean up, again, and then I'm heading to bed." As if to emphasize her point, she yawned and stretched.

On her way toward the bathroom, she paused in front of me. "You can talk to me about it, you know." She spoke quietly. "I can relate a little to what you went through, and I'm a great listener."

Before I could answer, she lifted on her tiptoes and planted a kiss on my lips. My hands rose to grasp her, but I clamped them back down at my sides. Then she disappeared down the hall, and I heard the shower running already when she opened the door.

"I can't believe our luck," said Felix, more to Andrus than me. "I didn't know what to expect, but she wasn't it."

Andrus nodded. "She'll keep you on your toes. Never underestimate her. And prepare to fall hard." He cast a glance over his shoulder at the bathroom door. "All of the strife leading up to this moment was worth it, if it means having her in our lives."

Felix laughed. "Always the poet."

Andrus elbowed him in the side. "Just wait. You'll be acting like a sappy, love-struck idiot soon enough."

Felix looked dubious. "So she's taken on some of my traits—"

"Unfortunately for her," said Andrus.

"Although I do hope she can tamp down that glow. That might give us away if we're trying to being covert," I said dryly.

Felix held up his hands. "Alright, take it easy." He waggled his eyebrows. "But I bet neither of you have ever made someone glow after sex."

I rolled my eyes. "Good to have you back, friend."

Giggles and Gareth's growl echoed from the bathroom just before distinctive slapping sounds and moans. We all cast glances at the hallway concealing the door from view. Felix laughed and Andrus shook his head with a lopsided grin.

"So much for being tired."

Felix snorted. "I'm sure she's exhausted. Gareth will just put her the rest of the way to sleep. He can benefit from her adventurous spirit. Might learn a few things."

We all laughed, and I reveled in the normalcy. We'd been separated for so long, but we were already falling back into our old routines like no time had passed at all.

"Did you take on any of her power?" Felix asked Andrus, who nodded.

"You'll notice things changing soon. For me it was the ability to pick up on languages easily. Gareth has some strange connection with Time that we haven't even come close to figuring out."

"If Arthur were here, his magick would've been a tremendous benefit to all of us. And combining it with her other power..." I said, a pang of grief hitting me. It was impossible to wrap my head around him being gone.

"Why are you speaking of Arthur in the past tense?" asked Felix.

The vampire made a strangled sound. "Shit." He swallowed, a lump working down his throat. "I don't know if Meg would want me to tell you without being able to explain her side."

"Andrus, what happened?"

Felix and Arthur had been friends longer than any of us. Inseparable.

The vampire still couldn't bring himself to say it, so I did. I was used to being the bad guy. "Arthur is dead."

Felix spluttered. "What? How?"

Andrus jumped in to explain after shooting me a furious glare. After he'd finished the story, Felix could only stare ahead in shock.

"Why didn't you tell me this immediately?"

"I'm sorry. It didn't occur to me. And Meg has no idea how close you two were. She's devastated by what she did. Learning this will crush her."

"Crush her?" said Felix. "I understand that she's our mate, and I understand Belsioch's manipulation. I don't blame her. But nor do you need to protect her feelings, or consider how she'll feel about something at the cost of being truthful with the rest of us."

Andrus lapsed into silence. "You're right. I'm sorry. We weren't hiding it from you, it just..."

Gareth and Meg wandered to the bedroom. I only heard one pair of feet and two voices, so I assumed the wolf was once again carrying their mate. Once Hadi joined us, things would get interesting. I wondered if Gareth's alpha had shown in any significant ways yet.

Felix closed his eyes and took a steadying breath. His Adam's apple bobbed and there was a quaver to his voice when he spoke. "I'm tired. I think I'll take one of the other bedrooms tonight."

Andrus nodded, looking guilty as Felix walked off.

"He needed to be told," I said.

Andrus rounded on me. "Not like that. Gods, Remi, what's wrong with you? Have you lost all sense of decency?"

"Decency has no place when the stakes are this high. Bluntness is expedient."

He scoffed. "I'm glad it sits well with you. But the rest of us actually care about each other."

That stung. My nostrils flared as I fought with my anger. "You don't know what I feel. Don't pretend that you do."

"You've got a funny way of showing it, then. You've done nothing but skulk and complain. Our mate keeps making an effort to make you feel welcome, but even she has her limits on compassion. Whatever they put you through in that dungeon still isn't an excuse to be a bastard to your *family*. Or have you forgotten that's what we are?"

"Family," I murmured. Rage and heartbreak roared to life within me and if I'd had my wings, I would've flown far from here. "Do not speak to me of family."

Even if Andrus hadn't known me as well as he did, he would've been able to tell a change of subject or outright retreat was in order. Whether it was the pain he saw in my eyes or a stubborn refusal to walk away, I'm not sure. But he nodded and fell silent.

He continued to eat while I busied myself moving around the room, getting my anger under control.

"So we find Hadi. And then what?" I asked.

Andrus raised his eyebrows. "You want to talk about this now?"

I shrugged. "No time like the present. I've been tagging along with no real idea of what's coming. I'd like to start putting together a plan."

He wanted to protest, but I stopped him. "I agree we need time to recuperate. The gods know I'm exhausted just from the running we've done so far. You and Gareth have been with her far longer and running the whole time."

Andrus nodded. "Except for our small reprieve right before the Hounds broke our door down."

I finally took a seat at the table, and we settled on an uneasy truce as I continued to pick at the food. I didn't know what I was eating, but it was delicious.

"How long has it been since you've eaten proper food?" asked Andrus.

"Gruel doesn't count as real?" I asked. "The king did send a special Christmas dinner one year. A pile of roasted rats."

"I'm sorry. How did you get caught?" he asked. "If you don't mind my asking."

"I'd rather not get into it," I said, casting my eyes down.

He nodded, and we slipped back into lighter conversation before he headed off to bed, joining Gareth and Meg in the master bedroom. I'm sure he would tell them all about my loss of control and one of them would try to pry the truth from me soon enough, but even after five years, the pain was too great. And how could I admit to this *family* that I had failed so spectacularly to protect another?

Chapter Six

Bel

They say wounded animals are the most dangerous. And a cornered one is the worst of all. After Death dealt me that blow, stealing half of my life force, I was left to crawl back to my base of operations, broken.

"I suppose now would be a bad time to say I told you so?" asked Risha, meeting me at the door of the lodge. The smug, self-satisfied smile on her face made me want to hurt her, badly. But I could do nothing, except crawl past her up the stairs and into the living room, crashing on the couch still stained with her brother's blood.

"You should have known better. I tried to—"

I lashed out, sending a whip of energy in her direction. It glanced across her face, doing minimal damage to her, but costing me greatly. I couldn't even summon the energy to scream, to howl. I was nothing but impotent rage.

Death would pay for this. They would all pay for this. If I had to burn down every last vestige, stronghold, link...

Anything and everything that they ever held dear would die at my hands.

Risha walked over to me calmly, one foot in front of the other, her light steps barely audible over the rushing of blood in my ears. "What do you want?" I asked. "To gloat? Congratulations. That bitch friend of yours survives once again. When the Titans break free and destroy the world, you and her can laugh together as you watch it burn."

"That's where you misunderstand. You can't seem to fathom that other people aren't driven solely by ego and power. I wanted to stop you from hurting other people. I was sick of the destruction that you wrought simply to raise yourself up on your throne. Did you even have a reason for it anymore, other than proving something to yourself? Making yourself feel all-powerful like you used to be?" She leaned in close. "Before the Titans proved otherwise?"

She smiled as I watched her out of the corner of my eye. "That's what it is, isn't it? The reason you never destroyed the Titans. You were forced to imprison them, because you aren't powerful enough to kill them. You never have been. That's your big secret. The one you're desperate to protect."

"You know nothing," I hissed.

"I know a lot more than you ever gave me credit for. Those final battles managed to weaken them enough that you could put them in their cage." She tilted her head to the side. "But those Titans that died weren't killed by you or your accomplices, were they? Those Titans sacrificed themselves to give their surviving brethren enough power to make it through their captivity. Because they knew even then what you refused to accept yourself."

Risha leaned in close. She smelled like cherries.

I hate cherries.

"You can't destroy primordial energy. It will outlast you every time. You can lock it away, limit its reach and power. But you—" She smiled. "Especially you—cannot ever destroy it. Your only hope in winning this fight is to keep them locked away forever. The one thing I can't figure out is how you're going to do it. Sure, removing every link they have is a good start. With the Desma gone, they would have no hope of returning as anything but shadows. But simply destroying them, and Meg, wouldn't accomplish a complete binding. So how do you plan to seal those gates forever?"

I closed my eyes. "Leave me."

I could hear her audible shrug. "I can wait. I've got time. You on the other hand..." I heard the creak of floorboards as she stood and backed away a couple of paces. "Once the Hounds catch up with you and find out that you don't have their prize anymore, it's pretty much over, isn't it?"

"Leave!" I put all the force behind that one word as I could, and still hated myself for how weak it sounded.

"Sleep tight." Risha retreated, heading down the stairs.

I was left in silence.

I didn't leave that couch for days, stewing in my own self-loathing, hating Meg and Death, and everyone else who stood in my way. But I would not win this fight unless I proved to them all that they were wrong.

Dragging myself outside was no small feat, and I moved as far into the woods as I could. I found a decent-sized clearing that looked comfortable enough to bed down in. I brushed away dead leaves and all the other detritus on the forest floor. Stripping off my clothes, I lay, back flat, making as much contact with the earth as I could. I drew power to me, drinking it up, siphoning it. I'd have to tread carefully, only take so much at once. Otherwise, I would leave a swath of dead forest around me. I'd hate to give myself away so quickly.

When I sensed the trees closest to me dying, I stopped. And then I slept, letting osmosis sip small amounts of power throughout my slumber.

I repeated the same procedure every day for weeks. None of the nephilim came looking for me. That's perfectly fine. They'll get theirs soon enough.

Once I finally felt strong again—even though my power was still just a shadow of what it had been—I made my way back out of the forest, climbing up the stairs of the lodge with a slow deliberateness. The door swung open silently, my steps heavy on the wooden floorboards. All around me was the aura of my indignation, undulating like flame. A few nephilim inside, speaking in hushed tones, froze when they saw me. Their eyes grew wide in fear.

"Lord Belsioch—" one stammered, but he didn't finish his sentence. I reached out, grabbing his neck and snapping it in one quick wrench, the bones reminding me of a chicken's, the way they crackled. The others scattered, dashing in all directions, but they weren't who I was looking for.

Risha was nearby. Still with my same measured movements, I made my way downstairs. She was sitting at her desk, pouring over some tome or other. She didn't even spare a glance when she heard me coming, but spoke half distracted. "Did you find—"

"Risha," I growled. Her head snapped up, but far from being alarmed, she leveled me with a measured gaze.

"It took you long enough. And you're still barely at two-thirds capacity. Death really walloped you bad."

This caught me by surprise. Why wasn't she afraid? Even in this state, I could still destroy her.

"You have a lot of nerve. At first I found it amusing when you seemed to find a spine, but now I simply find that I want to punish you. Severely." I took a menacing step forward. "What I did to your brother will seem like a mercy compared to what happens to you next."

"You are nothing. I have taken over this operation. These nephilim are mine to lead. We'll still ensure the Titans stay sealed, but I will make damn sure that you can't touch Meg ever again."

"Why do you choose to be so loyal to her?" I demanded, flecks of spittle flying from my mouth. "She was only ever a servant. A pawn. She had a singular purpose to serve. But we—" I shook my head. "My legions of nephilim were supposed to serve at my side, a king and his most trusted advisors, his counsel."

Risha tossed her head back and laughed with a cruel alacrity. "That's good. You actually believe your own bullshit. We were never anything to you except tools. We did your bidding without even bothering to question you, because that's what we were made for. That's what our parents did, and raised us to do. We served you. Never once did you see us as anything other than tools to forward your own aims. Half of them still believe in you, despite everything! Despite seeing your slow decay into madness."

She took a step forward of her own, bringing her within arm's reach of me. "Every ounce of glory you ever had has long since been overshadowed. You could've been great. We all believed that you would do amazing things, fix what had gone so horribly wrong. Unite everyone under the same banner. But it all went to your head, and your ego is so fragile that your loss broke you. You didn't know what to do with yourself. So you sank into brooding, and then over the years you fell into the same trap that all the other Ætherim have. Time."

She grinned sardonically. "Ironic, isn't it? Ageless, immortal beings. Rulers. Pillars of strength. Of power. Mere mortals can only stare in awe at beings that their minds can barely comprehend. Seeing it as worthy of worship. Of deification. They bowed at your feet, and you lapped it up. You drank in their praise, you accepted their offerings, their sacrifices, demanding ever more from them. The very thing that you claimed to go to war with the Titans over. All that power."

She shrugged. "And you just let it go to waste. You all built your ivory towers, your temples, your sanctuaries on the mountaintop. You isolated yourselves, even amongst your own kind. And you fell victim to your own false narratives. Convinced yourself of your own greatness, even though you no longer did anything to earn it. People were still willing to worship you. But you ignored them, you didn't think you needed them anymore. But you expected their allegiance when you came calling. What did you think would happen? When the world moved on? When you came down from your mountaintops, stepped out of your temples?"

She reached out and gripped my chin with sharp fingertips. "To find a world that left you behind."

I pulled away. "We never needed them. Our power is not contingent upon their belief in us," I said, disgusted at the implication.

"Maybe not. But you need to be needed. Everyone does. Even by one other person. You separated yourselves so far from humanity that eventually you lost your minds to delusion. Isolation. Because despite everything else, your minds are still just as susceptible as every other being, on this earth and others, to madness. You eschewed connection, because you thought it was below you. And now it's biting all of you in the ass. Now that you truly see what you've brought upon yourselves, you're pushing back. Desperate. Trying to claw your way back to the top and hold on for dear life."

I sneered. "If that's what you think, why are you still here at all? Just let it all go, let the chips fall where they may. Go hide in the Strangefells and wait for all this to blow over."

"Diminished capacity or not, you are still a very dangerous man. And like I said before, I have every intention of saving my friend from you."

I lunged forward, grabbing her around the throat. "Don't you dare call me that. I am no simple, pathetic man."

She simply smiled, her speech strained as my fingers clamped around her windpipe. "Could've fooled me."

A furious howl tore from me and I brought up my other hand, intent on wringing her neck just like I had the other, but she shot a hand to my chest and a burst of energy bloomed from her palm, crackling and snapping like a downed powerline before a heavy force crashed into me and I sailed across the room.

I bellowed and charged at her, but was brought up short by three figures appearing in front of me. Risha stood a head taller than they, looking at me with narrowed eyes and a triumphant smile.

"I told you a deal made with them would backfire on you. They were very upset to find that their prize had escaped."

The Hounds said nothing, but nodded their agreement. My heart pounded in my chest. I hadn't expected to see them so soon. I'd hoped—

"How would you even know that he escaped? Have you found one of the other Desma to return to the dungeon?"

They shook their heads in unison and spoke as one. "We were made aware that you cannot hold up your end of the bargain."

"Made aware how?"

"A little birdie told them," said Risha.

I snarled and tried to lunge for her, but the Hounds pushed me back. I licked my lips, sweat beading on my forehead. "Now hold on. It sounds like neither of us is currently upholding the agreement. Give me more time and I can get Death—"

"You never had him in the first place. He was there as a courtesy. Can you honestly not see that?" said one of the male Hounds, his lip curling in disgust. I still wasn't clear on who was who. I'm not even sure they knew their individual names, so used were they to being one singular entity.

I took a deep breath and squared my shoulders. "So where does this leave us? I'm still willing to work out an arrangement."

All three of them laughed, each Hound letting out a quick bark of sound before the next and the next, in an unnerving round. "You have nothing left to offer. It's amazing you can even stand right now. I think the only thing keeping you upright is your own righteous indignation," said the female.

"You shouldn't underestimate me," I warned.

The other male spoke. "Legion was no match for us. Even at your full power, you wouldn't stand a chance against us."

"Legion?" My interest piqued. I hadn't heard that name in millennia, but I'd known them once. Formidable, powerful. "Where did you run into them?"

The female waved her hand carelessly. "They had a nice little lair set up for themself in Paris. Under Notre-Dame of all places. I will admit, I was impressed by the arrangement. It was an extensive amount of control that they exerted over the populous. Their alchemist was a bit... extreme, but he had interesting ideas. Would've been interesting to see where it led."

"Did you kill them?" I asked.

They shook their heads. "Merely left them incapacitated. We would've hated to destroy a creature such as them."

I nodded slowly. "Then I suppose that's it. There's nothing left to say."

"No, there's not," they said in unison, taking synchronized steps forward.

I smiled, opening my hand and displaying the key that I'd had clenched in my fist. Risha's eyes widened, and her hand snapped to her throat, searching for what I'd stolen.

"He has a focus!" she shouted. "Hurry!"

But I was already drawing power. "Any point in the storm."

The portal blazed into existence and the Hounds leaped back, shielding their eyes. I yelled out a date at random and leaped through the gate just as their raking claws sliced my back and their howls filled the air.

CHAPTER SEVEN

Meg

The next morning, I woke early. I could tell something was wrong, even though the bond between Felix and me was still new and I was learning to distinguish between him and the others. When Andrus came to bed and Felix didn't follow, my suspicion was confirmed, but I wanted to give him time alone. The last thing I wanted was to become the pesky partner that couldn't stand for anyone to be angry. Especially given the mix of personalities, it was inevitable.

But now, with dawn creeping in under the window shades, I could tell Felix was awake. It took some doing, but I freed myself from my mates' arms. Thank the gods Gareth and Andrus didn't snore, otherwise we'd have a problem.

I crept into the hallway and knocked lightly on Felix's door. "Come in."

When I entered, Felix was sitting on the edge of his bed, head in his hands. He looked up and several emotions warred on his face before he settled on neutral.

"Mind if I sit down?" I asked.

He patted a spot next to him and I sat shoulder to shoulder with him. "What happened after I went to bed last night?"

He smirked. "You were still in the shower when it happened."

"Oh." I blushed. "You heard that, huh?"

"Hard not to," he chuckled. When I didn't relent in my steady stare, he looked resigned. "Andrus told me about Arthur."

"Shit," I said, heart dropping. "I'm sorry, I should've—"

"He explained the whole thing. I vaguely understand, but..." His voice cracked. "Arthur and I were close. We grew up together."

As if I didn't feel enough like a monster. I hadn't even considered that there might be deeper relationships within the Six. I wanted to comfort him, but I was the one who had taken Arthur from him. What could I hope to say or do to combat that?

Once again, the bond spoke louder than words ever could. All my guilt and grief poured forth, and Felix knew it was genuine. He wiped tears from my face and pulled me close, even as his own tears fell hot against my shoulder.

"I'm so sorry, Felix."

"I know."

Farah's people had put together a huge breakfast. She was waiting for us when we came down to the dining room, after leaving a gilded invitation card in our common area. My mates had managed wonderfully well at keeping me distracted and tired, but now all my worries came back.

I stopped in the doorway, holding her gaze.

"The message was delivered via proxy. If the Hounds haven't gotten the message already, I'll be shocked."

My breath burst from me as relief hit. The sudden endorphin rush made me lightheaded and if Gareth hadn't been coming in behind me to catch me, I would've fallen.

"Thank you," I said.

Farah nodded and sipped at the strong Turkish coffee that she favored. "So how was your evening? Productive, I hope?" she asked with a wink.

"Very," said Felix, giving me a side hug before taking a seat. The hurt I'd caused him wasn't gone by any stretch of the imagination, but we'd talked for over an hour, laying everything bare.

Farah eyed Remi suspiciously as he entered, quiet as always. The protrusions of bone from his reforming wings were becoming more prominent every day, and so was the pain he was in.

"But you didn't participate," she said. "Why?" Her Latin wasn't perfect, but the gargoyle could understand her just fine.

Remi gave her a casual glance, but he didn't answer. I could see that dangerous tick in Farah's eye that happens before she loses her temper, so I answered for him.

"I thought it would be too difficult to initiate two bonds at once. Remi bowed out."

"Did he?" said Farah. She didn't believe a word of it, but she let it go.

Once we were all gathered and tucking into breakfast, Farah asked, "What are your plans for the day?"

I looked at the others. "We were waiting to hear about Hadi. But now that we know the Hounds won't be after him…"

"Might I suggest a shopping trip?" Farah wrinkled her nose at my men. "Those sweatpants aren't proper attire."

"Then why do you have so many of them?" asked Remi. I kicked him under the table, and he jumped, blinking at me before forcing a begrudging apology out of his mouth. "I meant no offense. We are grateful for your hospitality."

Farah pursed her lips. "Yes, well." Her eyes flicked to me. "That mystery stash you built here is still in the same spot."

I chuckled and shook my head. "Of course you know about that."

"Stash?" asked Gareth.

"A treasure hoard," I grinned. "Nothing too exciting, just cash."

"She hid the gold somewhere else more personal," said Farah. She raised her eyebrows at Remi. "You should try to find it."

I choked on the sip of orange juice I'd taken while the others—excluding Remi—snickered.

"What we're planning for? That you needed to hide money?" Andrus asked between bites. He'd already polished off a whole plate of food and showed no signs of slowing.

I looked at Farah for the go ahead. "I never told you how Farah and I met."

"You mean how I caught you stealing from me?" she asked, albeit with a good-natured smile.

That peaked Andrus's interest. "What's this?"

"My keepers brought me here for an event. Farah was hosting the annual ball that brings all the oldest families out of their mansions and into one place."

"You make it sound so droll," said Farah.

"It is," I challenged. She just shrugged.

"I was bored, so went snooping. I was in my full rebellion phase at the time. They hadn't broken my spirit yet."

"Who were your keepers?" asked Remi. "And how could they let you wander the home of a sphinx unattended."

"This time you raise a great question," said Farah. "My thoughts were the same."

"I was raised by the Gieses."

Grim looks were shared all around. Mine wasn't the only life they had fucked with. The Gieses made it their mission to treat people like garbage every chance they got. The Ætherim they descended from were the type that lived in deep, dark forests, and built fences made of the bones of their enemies. I'm not sure I'd be able to reconcile that with the Titans' choice to send me to them. If they had been concerned with my well-being at all, why trust a family with a reputation like theirs?

"Anyway. I liked shiny things. And I found shiny things."

"And you got caught," said Felix.

"I was none too pleased." Farah's lip curled. "The Gieses didn't even make excuses. They wanted me to punish her."

"What?" Gareth's tone was low.

"At first, I was all for it. Her obstinance came off as arrogance. If I hadn't bothered to speak with her, I would've taken action. But it was clear she was being mistreated and finding any way she could to fight back." She shook her head. "I was far angrier with them than with Meg. And I made that abundantly clear."

"So I got to hang out with Farah every once in a while so she could check in with me. They may have claimed the Titans as allies, but Farah was a real threat staring them down that the

Titans couldn't protect them from." I didn't care if it was cruel or coldhearted; I was glad they were dead.

"If I ever wanted to escape their house, I'd need funds. So I built up a stash."

"Which she thought she was keeping secret from me," the sphinx chuckled.

"Farah was the only friend I had, until Bel..." Until Bel murdered my keepers and isolated me from everyone else.

Farah's disgust was plain. "That son of a bitch." She cocked her head. "How did you get away from him? And with the Hounds involved?"

I shared a look with the others, unsure if I should go into details. I trusted Farah, but there were plenty of other people listening that I didn't. Andrus shook his head slightly.

"A fluke, dumb luck."

Again, Farah wasn't fooled, but she understood. "Well... you'll have to celebrate then. Mardi Gras is just getting started."

"We can allow ourselves one night out on the town," I said. "It'd be a shame to miss it."

After breakfast, Farah pulled me aside. "What aren't you telling me?"

"Are you sure we won't be overheard?" I asked, glancing around us.

Farah frowned at the implication that her staff was untrustworthy, but she nodded. "Let's take a walk. The garden is lovely right now."

She led me out back of the house to a sprawling vista that was not within New Orleans's city limits. She'd played a little fast-and-loose with dimensional restrictions and expanded her backyard to several dozen acres of gardens.

"Wow," I said. "I missed this place."

She looped her arm through mine. "It's good to have you back. You don't know how many times I thought about trying to steal you away from Bel."

I stopped. "Really? That would've been suicide."

She frowned. "Hence, why I didn't. But I felt like I'd abandoned you."

"No. You gave me a place to call home. Without these visits, I would've... I don't know. Fallen apart, at the very least. And even when Bel had me completely snowed, I always knew you would be there if I needed you."

Farah schooled her expression, but I still caught the softening of her face. I'd almost coaxed a full smile from her.

"So. Belsioch?" she asked. We turned the corner into a shaded grotto surrounded by flowering vines.

"We're working with Death."

"What?" she asked, whirling to face me. "Death?"

I tugged her along to keep walking, not wanting to make a big deal out of it. "Yes. I already told you about Bel sending the Hounds after us and Death being their payment."

"The fool," Farah spat.

I laughed. "Agreed. Farah, let me tell the story."

She sniffed. "Fine."

"Death was playing Bel the whole time. The Hounds caught us and delivered us to him, and when they left to look for the others, Death made his offer. He's building a team of some kind. He says he's not even sure what for."

"And you trust this?"

I hesitated. "Yes and no. But I'm still confident it was the only option."

She nodded.

"Bel was in the midst of trying to kill us, but it wasn't working. Death escaped his prison cell and stole half of Bel's life force."

Farah inhaled sharply. "You don't say." She glanced back at the house. "I guess I can't blame you for not wanting to share that information around others. If word got out, there would be no end to people jockeying for position."

"This will be hard enough without Bel 2.0 trying to set up shop."

We walked a little more in silence, enjoying the day. The flowers were fragrant, their heady perfume filling the air as only the slightest breeze blew by.

"So what is your plan?" asked Farah.

"We don't have one," I admitted. "Besides find Hadi."

Her brow was furrowed, her eyes distant. I recognized the look. Sphinxes—on top of their well-known love for riddles and quick, ferocious tempers—have one other ability that makes them great to know. They are vast repositories for knowledge. They collect it, keep it, protect it. She was sifting through her mental library. "I think you should make contact with the Titans."

For a minute, I thought I'd misheard her. "Why? And how?"

"You are so close to the end of your journey, but you don't know where to go next, or what to do, besides the obvious. They'll be able to guide you. To make sure you're not missing anything. You can't afford to fall short now."

"I can hear you're brimming with confidence," I said wryly.

"I won't apologize for being realistic." She fixed me with a stern look. "Do you remember Nichelle?"

"The swamp witch?" I nodded. "Yeah. And I'm sure she remembers me, too. Not fondly." The last time we'd met, I'd stuck a knife in her gut and took off with an old grimoire that had been in her family for ages. Risha had needed it, and Bel told me to acquire it by any means necessary. That our mission would be compromised without it.

"She can get you there. To Tartarus."

"Woah. I can't just reach them in trance?"

"You won't be able to get past the gates. If you could go there in your mind only, every occult practitioner that wanted another notch on their taboo bedpost would try it. It has to be your physical body or your astrally projected soul."

I frowned. "Okay. That's fine, but I've astrally projected before. Why can't I do it myself?"

"You need to be dropped *within* the gates of Tartarus. Nichelle is great with soul travel. She'll be able to get you there safely."

"Uh..."

"At least try to work something out with her. You need to find a way there. Don't risk everything falling apart now."

I chewed my lip. "Okay. I'll give it a shot." We were passing through an arbor surrounded by jasmine. I held out my hand to let my fingers sift through the delicate flowers, releasing more of their fragrance in the air.

"So are you going to tell me how you accomplished getting that message to the Hounds?" I asked. "Some kind of secret cabal? A network of spies?"

Farah laughed. "Nothing like that. I believe you know the messenger."

I raised an eyebrow.

"Risha, I think her name is."

"You spoke to Risha? Is she okay? Is she—" I chewed on the words, wondering if I even wanted to know. Is she still on my side? Was she ever?

"Our conversation was brief, but I'd heard that Bel was turning on his subordinates. In the few times we've spoken since Bel "saved" you, you mentioned that you and she were friends. I took a chance. She was grateful for the information. You still have a friend in that one."

Tears were welling up in my eyes. Farah spotted it and scowled. "Stop that."

"Nope. You're getting a hug."

"Don't you dare."

"It's happening." I opened my arms and moved toward her, but she backed up and raised her hand, pointing.

"Megiste," she said, eyes narrowed.

I laughed. "One of these days, you'll let me love you."

She scoffed, but her mouth twitched at the corners. Farah jerked her head toward the house. "Go plan your night out. Promise me you'll take the time to have some fun. You deserve it."

"Yes, ma'am."

Bourbon Street was hopping as every tourist in the city clogged the sidewalks and every bar had a band playing. The sun had only just set, and my men were looking around in fascination, various levels of disbelief on their faces. Felix was already getting the benefit of the language lexicon through our new bond, but

Remi was still the odd one out. Something was weighing on him even more heavily than usual. Andrus had mentioned things got heated when he spoke to Remi of his past, family in particular, but that was it.

I'd taken them all to a menswear outlet—a more arduous process than you'd imagine, since they weren't used to fast fashion and clothing of all sorts at their fingertips. They'd all chosen various shades of black and jewel- toned button-up shirts.

The result was four men in suits that, while not tailored, still fit them well enough to make me drool like an idiot when they came out of the dressing rooms.

"Modern fashion works for you."

Felix did a strut on an imaginary catwalk, and I don't think it was in mockery of modern- day habits. I think he was just a natural preener.

I was surrounded by four excessively handsome gentlemen, all at least a foot taller than me, most of them two. As we moved through the crowds, it was amazing how many people stopped in their revels to watch us go by.

"Is it always like this?" asked Felix.

"Yes and no. Same atmosphere, but Mardi Gras always brings in the extra crowds. I know it's overwhelming, but if you just let yourself get lost in it, I promise it's worth it. We're safe for the time being. Let's enjoy ourselves."

Felix looked like he had doubts, but nodded anyway.

The thing that struck me most as we continued was that they were impervious to the attention. No matter how many doe-eyed glances they received from women passing by—and not a few men—they rebuffed all of it. And nobody got angry, because it was clear these men weren't being rude on purpose. They just didn't get what the fussing over them was about.

Only one thing made me doubt my choice to bring them here. Remi was getting as much attention as the rest of them, but it wasn't all positive. He had scars all over his face and neck from his time in the dungeons, and the most common reaction to him was staring or shying away. Like they thought he was dangerous. I mean, he was. Very much so. But not unless it was called for.

There were still many mysteries to unravel about him, but when a woman gasped and stumbled in fright after she bumped into him, I threaded my fingers through his and he clasped them tight. He looked at me curiously and I just smiled up at him and kept walking.

"So we're heading to find this friend of yours later tonight?" asked Gareth.

"Hopefully," I said.

They gave me suspicious glances, but didn't question it further. I know it was stupid not to tell them the whole story, but they would overreact and forbid it. I still wouldn't listen, and they'd follow me anyway. At least this way we could avoid the beating of chests and declarations of protection. I didn't *need* their protection, dammit.

There was one more reason for bringing them down here that I was looking forward to sharing with them. The next street over had some great restaurants, and I couldn't wait to see their faces the first time they tried jambalaya, red beans and rice, or crawfish étouffée. And if we could get up early enough, maybe we'd go out for fresh beignets.

I had my eye on a bar up ahead. It was pretty packed, but the band was amazing.

Andrus eyed it warily. "As a fair warning, I haven't danced in at least a thousand years. Will that be a problem?"

A couple passing by at just that moment shot us a confused look.

I laughed. "I'm not very good either. We're just here to enjoy the music."

We approached the bar and people moved aside for our group. There was plenty of whispering in our wake. They probably thought one of the men was a movie star and he'd brought his entire entourage.

I bypassed the bar. A small table had opened up, a high top, and I made my way over to it. As I climbed up into the chair—I always hated barstool-style seating—I glimpsed our reflection from the mirror behind the bar.

Suddenly, I realized what we look like to other people. Here I was, a small woman, not too shabby, but certainly not a perfect ten like the guys surrounding me. They could've been models or international assassins. I was so out of place with them, my natural resting bitch face not helping matters. People would assume that I was a spoiled rich girl that bought escorts for the night. Maybe I could make up a story about being a mafia boss's daughter. That would fit and make the scenario a little more believable.

I caught Gareth's eye in the mirror, and he winked at me, wrapping his hand around my side and letting it rest on my hip. I shifted uncomfortably, and he backed off.

"What's wrong?" he asked into my ear, the music pounding.

I shook my head. "Nothing. I'm just being a self-conscious weirdo."

"About what?" The others were looking at me now and I felt heat rising in my cheeks. Being heavily considered by the direct gazes of four gentle giants with hero complexes was daunting.

"It's nothing." I tried to laugh it off, too embarrassed to say it out loud. I kind of forgot the whole "bond" thing for a minute.

They figured it out pretty quick.

"Meg," Andrus said, eyes sparkling as he tried to tamp down his laughter. "You have no idea how beautiful you are. We may be getting gawked at, but most eyes land on you."

I was about to tell him it was obviously because they were judging me, but he continued.

"It's because they want you—"

Gareth growled and moved closer. I rolled my eyes simultaneously with Andrus and Remi.

"—or because they're curious. Your allure draws people in."

"Or they're curious about how *all this* happens," said Felix with a wicked smile, motioning at our group. "And I don't blame them. It is something to behold."

My mates chuckled as Remi stared at the dance floor intently, like he was studying the people on it.

"Oh, my gods, stop," I pleaded, my face on fire. "You've made your point."

The song ended and applause thundered from the patrons. The next song up was a slow jam and people coupled up.

Remi smiled and took my hand. "Not yet, we haven't."

CHAPTER EIGHT

Meg

He bowed and offered his hand. I laughed awkwardly, gaze darting around the room. "That's not necessary."

Remi raised his head and looked me in the eye. "It is. Let's show them all that we are unapologetically us. And unafraid." He shrugged with a grin. "And I'd like everyone here to witness your beauty in my arms."

My heart melted, and I placed my hand in his. The gargoyle drew me to my feet, and we moved to the dance floor, people moving aside once again to give us room.

He held me close as we swayed to the music and the people surrounding us just fell away in the background. Nothing else existed but us. His warmth, the heartbeat thrumming in his chest as I rested my head against him, the callouses on his fingers as his hand landed at the small of my back, the occasional light stroke of his touch sending shivers through me.

The song ended all too soon and in the lull between songs, I glanced up at him. He was staring down at me with a gentle smile, the calmest and—dare I say—happiest I'd seen him in the little time I'd known him.

A new song started up, much livelier, and I took his hand, heading back for the edge of the dance floor, but he didn't move. I looked back and a small yelp escaped my throat as he tugged at me, pulling me back to him in a spin. A glint of mischief took up in his gaze, and I laughed right before he launched into a dance. He'd been studying the people on the dance floor alright.

You would never have guessed that I'd just pulled him forward from medieval France with the modern dance moves he was putting down. And if he could move his hips like that here, I could only imagine...

I shook my head as I noticed his pupils dilate, sensing the stirrings of lust within me even without the bond. He left me breathless after a series of spins, dipping me back so far my hair swept the floor before he pulled me upright, spun me again, and dipped me low on the opposite side. I crashed back into his chest, giggling and lightheaded.

To my surprise, Andrus appeared behind Remi and clapped his hand on the gargoyle's shoulder. Remi looked around and Andrus jerked his head toward our table before taking Remi's place. He gave a conciliatory nod and walked off as Andrus pulled me close, his lips brushing the shell of my ear. "Can't let him have all the fun."

"I thought you didn't dance," I teased.

"I just said it's been a while."

Without further warning, Andrus picked up right where Remi had left off, both of us breathlessly dipping, spinning, and grinding together through the next two songs. When another slow song came along, Gareth stepped in, and Andrus stepped out.

"This is the only kind of dancing I'm capable of," he said, chuckling. "I didn't want to miss out." I breathed in the woodsy cologne he'd bought on our shopping trip. It was a perfect scent for him, and I let myself be enveloped by it, molding against his body like we were two halves of a whole. An overwhelming sensation of love poured over me through the bond, so strong that I gasped. His arms wrapped around me tighter and in my mind, I heard him say, *I told you, love. You've ruined me.*

I looked up at him and pulled his face down to mine, just a brief, light kiss. And then the song ended. He sighed heavily and let me go. Another song began, much more upbeat. "That's my cue," he said, just as Felix appeared, a wide grin on his face.

"Finally," said Felix. "I get to show off." He held out his hand and waggled his eyebrows. "Are you ready?"

I slapped my hand into his with a smile, and we were off. Gods. Felix wasn't kidding when he said he was good, and he led so well that I looked damn good, too. He didn't even have to use illusion to supplement his talent. Never underestimate a fae on the dance floor.

People backed up to make a circle around us, cheering us on. The song crescendoed and Felix tossed me in the air, guiding me back to the floor. My toes had no sooner touched the ground when he spun me wildly into a low dip, sweeping me all the way around and jerking me back into his arms as the song ended. We only had eyes for each other, flushed and panting for breath as thunderous applause sounded around us.

When the next song started, the spell was broken and he released me, sweeping a hand through his hair which had come loose, tendrils hanging into his face. He smiled, almost shy now that his display was over.

"That was amazing!" I said, laughing.

"I was highly motivated," he replied, trying to brush off the compliment even though his pride swelled through the bond. His fingers tilted my chin up, and he captured my lips in a deep, passionate kiss that had me swooning. Quicker than I could protest, he scooped me up in his arms and carried me off the floor, back toward our group.

The other three men were shaking their heads, forcing scowls onto their faces that threatened with each passing second to revert to smiles. "Way to make us look bad," said Andrus.

"Always," said Felix with a wink.

The large red digital clock face on the wall behind the bar caught my eye. "We should get going."

"To find more adventure?" asked Remi. "Or did you have something else in mind?" An innocent enough question, but his tone implied much more. I circled around the table and stood close.

"That depends. Are you ready for something else?"

He took my hand with his own, raising the other to brush my cheek. "Soon."

I nodded. "In that case." I turned to include the others. "Who's hungry?"

Felix immediately made it dirty. "Hungry for…"

"Food," I clarified, exasperated. But I'd be lying if I said I wasn't tempted.

"Ah. Right, right," he said. "I could eat." He winked at me.

I'd been right to suspect that they would enjoy the food scene here. They were dubious at first, so I ordered a nice selection of my favourite dishes the south had to offer and got family-sized servings of each one. We had it all. Spice, heat, flavor, fried everything, and plenty of sweet tea to wash it down.

The men devoured their first plates in about five minutes, all doubt vanishing. I've never had more fun watching people eat. Felix was probably the only one who was used to eating for pleasure instead of just sustenance.

"You've got some cheese in your beard." I handed Gareth a napkin with a somewhat smug grin and pointed to the corner of his mouth.

He sheepishly wiped at his face. "Got carried away, huh?"

"Not at all. I think you just won my argument for me—bear jerky is gross."

He barked a surprised laugh. "Yes. I will never look at bear jerky again."

Andrus, wiping sticky sauce off his hands, nodded his agreement. "Between that marvelous indoor plumbing and—" he motioned at the spread on the table. "This time is pretty great. Despite a few setbacks." He shot a look at the television in the corner. None of them had taken to modern electronics yet, and this was the '80s. Their heads might explode when they saw a smartphone for the first time.

"What is this?" asked Remi, adding more gravy to his plate of sliced smoked ham.

"Red-eye gravy," I said.

"Red-eye gravy," he repeated. He was still speaking a mix of Ancient Greek, Latin and Medieval French, all of which were preventing him from saying the words easily. He took another bite and savored it. "You know what, doesn't matter. I'm calling it bloody delicious."

"It's got coffee in it, so it's nice and bitter," I said.

"Just like him," said Felix.

Remi joined in the laughter, and I squeezed his knee under the table, sharing a private smile with him.

Andrus caught me staring at him as he finished his second plate, reaching for the spoon and more cheesy grits. "What? Something on my face?"

"No." My grin made him do a double take.

"What's that look for?" He chuckled. "I suddenly feel like I'm on the menu."

"Did her teeth get sharper?" asked Gareth.

I laughed. "I'm just really glad you're adjusting so well. I was worried all this would be too overwhelming."

"It is," said Andrus. "But the abilities you've given me have helped a lot. You being by my side makes everything a little less daunting. If we can survive the Hounds, Legion, Bel, a volcano... Loud noises and bright lights are the least of my worries. Especially when this food is available."

"Agreed," said the others.

"Can I get y'all anything else?" the server asked, sidling up to the table and laying a hand on Gareth's massive forearm. Her thumb stroked one of his tattoos.

I coughed, choking on a laugh as Gareth looked at the woman's hand, back at the woman and then to me with an eyebrow peaked. "This is pretty forward, isn't it?"

The server's hand stilled and she pulled it back, glaring daggers of jealousy at me. "I'll just bring your check, then."

Gareth reached over and took my hand and the server's face soured to a dangerous level of pucker before she marched away.

I laughed. "I'm glad we already got our food though, otherwise she'd probably spit in it."

He raised my hand to his mouth and brushed his lips over the back of my knuckles, nostrils flaring as he scented the desire rolling off me.

"Let's get the errand done, so we can get back to the house. We need some undisturbed time with our mate."

I looked at Remi, and he nodded, reaching over to take my other hand. Felix and Andrus were no less invested in this turn of conversation and when the server returned with our check, she huffed loudly, slapped it on the table and stalked off.

"Okay," I said, sliding out of the booth. My knees were threatening to turn to jelly with three mates, and one soon-to-be, turning me into a wanton puddle of need with their stares. "You have to cool it. I can't focus when you're zapping me with panty-dropper vibes."

I pulled some cash from my purse and dropped it on the table. There wasn't a crumb of food left, and my men followed me out of the restaurant. As we walked, Felix's hand rested on my ass and he leaned in. "That's the point." His fingers deftly lifted my skirt and skimmed along my ass cheek, forcing a shuddering breath from my mouth.

"Quit it, I'm serious," I said, smacking him lightly on the chest.

He sighed and moved his arm up to circle my waist. "Very well then. It'll just give us more time to plan out what we're going to do to you when we get back to our room."

I heard various agreements from the three behind me and I squeezed my thighs together to combat the sudden throbbing.

"We'll have to catch a taxi."

We headed back to Bourbon Street, which was crawling with cabs. There weren't any vans, so I had no choice but to hail an average sedan. It was going to be a tight squeeze. I leaned in the window before we went to the trouble of piling in, to make sure he'd take us.

"Where to?" asked the driver.

"We need to go to Bayou Lafourche."

"Seriously? That's at least a forty-five-minute drive, depending on where you want me to drop you off."

"We'll pay extra for your trouble." I held up a couple hundred in cash.

He smiled. "Hop in."

Gareth took the front seat, and it was a toss-up whose lap I'd be sitting on in the back. I ended up choosing Felix. I didn't know the specifics, but staying close to the mate I'd just bonded with always felt the most secure, comfortable.

He shrugged and put the car in gear. The road rumbled past as country music hummed on the radio.

"Y'all from Lafourche?"

"No. Visiting someone," I said.

"Pretty late for a visit," said the driver, dubious. He caught my eyes in the mirror.

"She's a night owl." Take it or leave it, that's the only explanation he was getting.

There was a bumpy stretch, and the driver cursed as we hit several potholes in a row.

"Damn city needs to fix this shit," he grumbled, but anything else he said I didn't notice. What I did notice was Felix growing hard beneath me. I felt his exhale of breath on the back of my neck as his fingers grazed my skin, gathering my hair and moving it aside to place a kiss behind my ear before he said, "Sorry. Damn potholes." But he didn't sound sorry in the least.

Two can play that game. Between the dancing, the good food and the rush of confidence, it had me acting out of character. I never would've done anything like this with a stranger around before, but right now I didn't care.

I ground my ass against him, and he inhaled sharply. The others stiffened, their eyes turned toward us. Luckily, the driver remained oblivious, still furious about the quality of the roads.

I moved again and Felix's arm snaked around my waist, holding me firmly to him as I continued to move.

"You asked for it, princess," he said into my ear. His other hand dipped under the waistline of my skirt and panties both, sliding through my folds and gathering my wetness before spreading it up to circle my clit.

A gasp threatened to tear loose, but I swallowed it. Felix deftly worked me toward my peak so fast my head spun. I struggled to keep my breathing steady, switching my hips against him.

I knew I wouldn't be able to remain silent when I came and as my body tightened, Andrus leaned over and covered my mouth with his own, his kiss fevered. My orgasm tore through me and I moaned into his mouth. As I came down, still locked in a devouring kiss with Andrus, he took every whimper and sigh.

When I snapped out of the haze of pleasure, I noticed Gareth was distracting the driver, asking him questions and pointing at things on either side of the road. Andrus nipped my lower lip and backed away, his fingers caressing my jaw as he did.

Felix pulled his hand away and stared nonchalantly out of the window like nothing had happened, a grin on his face.

We were nearing the bayou, so I gave turn-by-turn directions. The populated areas fell away as we moved farther from the main body of water. The dark and humid wetlands seemed to swallow the headlights the closer we got to Rathborne Swamp.

"Here," I said, pointing toward the mouth of an old dirt road.

The driver did a double take. "You want me to drop you here? Y'all are fools if you want to go out there dressed like that. Weren't you visiting someone? Ain't nobody around."

"This is it," I said firmly. I handed him the cash, and we got out of the car. The second we closed the doors, he sped off, and we were alone in the swamps of Louisiana, in the middle of the night. A full moon lit our way, and there wasn't another soul in sight. A perfect time to meet a swamp witch.

I realized my mistake five minutes in. "I'm an idiot. Why didn't I bring sensible shoes? And bug spray?" The mosquitos were making a meal out of my exposed skin. Remi offered me his suit jacket, to at least save my arms, but then it was a toss-up for what was worse. Getting eaten by bugs, or sweltering in the humidity.

"I've had easier hikes through mountains," Andrus grumbled. He cursed when he stepped in a puddle. "Remind me to check my feet for leeches later."

I wrinkled my nose. "That's a horrifying picture."

Deep water surrounded us on both sides. The trees hung thick with Spanish moss and the croaking of the frogs was ominous instead of comforting. Crickets, owls, all the favorite nighttime sounds, became something else in this place. It was beyond spooky.

Even though I knew where I was going, it didn't make it any easier to calm my nerves. Through the moss and lichen, smoky forms and figures walked in the mist. The ghosts of this bayou were out in force tonight. A woman crossed our path, a shimmering humanoid form that was barely holding together. She looked toward us with sad eyes before she dissipated.

"Do you see those too?" asked Gareth.

"Yes," I said. As we walked farther, the ghosts lined up along the road, watching us pass. Others continued to wander in the background, only a shadow of a memory, repeating the last minutes of their lives.

I hated this ability. To see spirits, trapped, and not able to do anything to help them, even though they thought I could, just because I could see them. It's not as easy as helping someone with their unfinished business and hoping they pass over peacefully. Or ringing a few bells and calling yourself an exorcist.

Necromancers are the only ones that can send people into the afterlife, regardless of how they got trapped here, and I wasn't one. I may have had somewhat similar abilities, but that's where the parallels ended. Although, I wondered if—

Something large moved through the water, dragging itself onto land with a wet sliding sound. "Crocodiles?" asked Felix.

"Alligators. Not as big, and they should leave us alone if we steer clear."

"How big?" Gareth asked.

"Probably no more than fourteen feet, max," I said. Even in the dark, I could see him shiver at the thought.

"What, you don't care for prehistoric lizard monsters?" I asked, teasing.

"Not in the slightest," he answered.

"Nobody warned me there'd be monster hunting," griped Felix.

"We should be fine if we stay on the road. The snakes might get us though. Or the spiders." I reached and tickled the back of Remi's neck. He didn't even flinch.

"Was that supposed to scare me?" he asked, grinning.

"I mean, I was hoping for a bit of a startle."

"You're going to have to try harder than that," he said.

"I think he just issued a challenge," said Gareth.

"He realizes Felix is back with us, right?" asked Andrus.

"I take it you're the trickster of the group?" I asked him.

Felix brushed his coat lapels. "I've been known to play a good joke every now and again."

The other three men groaned.

Up ahead was a house, just visible through the trees. "There it is," I said, pointing.

The others paused to look, and Gareth frowned. "That's not terrifying at all. Was this all a hoax so you could lure us here and murder us?"

"Guess we'll find out," I said with a casual shrug.

He chuckled, moving close and taking my hand. "As long as yours is the last face I see, I'm fine with that."

"Wow. Way to make me feel bad about it. I guess the murder plot's off now."

Just peeking through the trees—you'd miss it if you didn't know to look for it—was a small wooden walkway that stretched over the water and connected the stilt house to dry land. The moment I stepped onto the old and rickety dock, everything went quiet.

CHAPTER NINE

Meg

Behind me, my men stilled, waiting.

"I'm pretty sure this is just a security measure she's taken. I hope."

"Megiste." A clear voice with a heavy accent called me from the front door. "I didn't think I'd be seeing you again." Her tone was less than welcoming.

Remi leaned down to speak into my ear. "I thought you said you were friends?"

"I said I knew her. You inferred that we were friends."

He growled. "What did we just walk into?"

"It's fine. She might be a little pissed off at me, but—"

A blast of magick zipped over our heads, missing Andrus by inches. A deliberate shot across our bow.

"Come on, Nichelle! That was ages ago. I thought you'd be over it by now!" I called. "It wasn't personal."

Another magick burst, closer this time. I felt the air rush as it flew over my head. "Just hear me out, please! I just want to talk!"

"Get out of here, and never show your face again," she said, sending a wave of magick crashing toward us. It broke on us, and I felt nauseous, followed by dizziness so severe I had to grab a nearby tree for support.

"I think we should listen to her," said Felix. "Seems like she means business."

"I need your help!"

"Like you did last time?" Fire erupted on the water, surrounding her cabin with the orange glow.

"Bel talked to me into it. I know that's not an excuse—"

"Damn right it's not. I want my grimoire back!" The fire crept closer to us, the shapes of men armed with swords forming in the flames.

"I can't do that, at least not right now. I got away from Bel."

The warriors paused in their advance. "Then who's with you?" Nichelle called.

"These are my mates. They're good men. They won't harm you." She fell silent. "Please. I need your help."

After a moment, the flames died and the swamp witch turned, moving back into her cabin. But she left the door open.

"Come on," I said, taking cautious steps forward.

"Are you sure about this?" Andrus asked.

"She has a temper, but usually once the flames go out, she's fine."

"At least let one of us go first," said Gareth.

"No." My tone was firm. "I just need you to back me up. I've got this."

He looked like he might argue but changed his mind. I continued up the boardwalk, watching with trepidation as glowing eyes moved in close, peering at us out of the water.

When I reached the front door, there was a slight resistance as I stepped inside. "What did I just step through?" I asked.

Nichelle was sitting by the fireplace. Her dark hair was as wild as her eyes. Madness had taken her before, and she was always one step away from it happening again. Isolation does horrible things to a person.

As her power grew stronger, she moved deeper into the swamps. She has a lot of family here, descended from one of the oldest Creole families in the area, and all of them are magi. But they can't convince her to leave. "If you had any protections on you, you don't anymore. While you're in my house, you're at my mercy."

Considering what happened last time, I certainly didn't blame her for taking extra precautions.

The four men joined me in the small cabin, but far from making me feel more secure, it felt like there might be a problem if I had to move quickly.

"So what can I do for you?" she asked, a wry grin on her face.

"I'm planning a family reunion, and I need your help to get me there."

Nichelle's eyebrows rose. "Are you serious? Why the hell would you want to do that?"

"Yes, Meg," asked Gareth, his tone patronizing. "Why would you want to do that?"

I shot him a warning glare. We would discuss this later, I guaranteed.

"I have very specific questions that only they can answer."

"The Desma can't answer them?" asked Nichelle. "They were closer to the Titans than anyone."

I shook my head, looking at the others. "The specifics were never shared with them. Maybe the Titans thought it would be self-explanatory, but it's not. We can't afford to make mistakes this close to the end," I said, parroting Farah's words to me earlier.

"And I suppose there's a specific way you want to get there?"

"In spirit," I confirmed.

"Isn't that the same as when you go into a trance?" asked Remi.

Nichelle answered for me. "Trance will only get your mind there. She needs me to yank her soul from her body and send that to Tartarus."

"Forgive my bluntness, but are you insane?" Andrus asked me. "That's an incredible risk. For what?"

"We have no plan. Gareth admitted to me that he doesn't know how this is supposed to go down, so I'm guessing none of you do either." I waited for them to contradict that. Nobody did. "So we either waste time trying to figure it out, or go right to the source and ask."

"Did you come up with this plan on your own?" asked Felix.

I paused. "No. Farah suggested it. Why?"

"It does seem drastic," he said. "Are you sure—"

"Farah wouldn't betray me," I said, staring him down and daring him to refute it. I'd made plenty of mistakes, but trusting Farah wasn't one of them.

"If I do this for you, what will you give me in return?" Nichelle asked.

I broke my eye contact with Felix. "What do you want?"

She considered. "How about a favor? Nothing really good is coming to mind right now. I don't want to waste my shot at getting something good out of you."

"No favors," said Felix instantly.

He had a point. What she could do with a favor, and he, as fae, could, were two very different things. But I had no desire to offer her one, regardless.

"No favors," I asserted.

"Then you can leave," she said.

My lips pursed. "What if I put constraints on it? Limits? Would you accept that?"

She shrugged. "Within reason."

Felix grunted. "Still no." He looked at me. "Farah can help us. Her magic is even more potent than this witch's, and it was her idea in the first place."

Nichelle stood. "Farah's magick is nothing compared to mine."

"But she could give it a shot. I'd be happier trying that, than letting my mate give you a favor," said Felix.

The swamp witch scoffed. "You'll be lucky if she gets you halfway to your destination."

Felix shrugged. "Very well then." He turned and ushered me ahead of him.

Nichelle's face twisted and she waved her hand. The door slammed shut in our faces. "I will not have you come in here, to my home, and insult me like that!"

The elf remained calm. "It wasn't an insult. It was merely a fact. We'll take our chances with the sphinx. And I imagine if she does do the job well, it might tarnish your record a bit, no?"

The conjurer licked her lips nervously. "Empty threats."

Felix said nothing, just looked at her expectantly.

Nichelle growled. "Fine. I'll do it."

I closed my eyes within a circle of stones, bones, and nubs of candles guttering in their pools of wax. Herbs burning in a brazier covered me with thick smoke. The worried faces of my mates were barely visible through it as Nichelle started her incantations. The firelight flickered and an owl screeched in the distance.

Then I felt like I was floating. I wanted to open my eyes, but the potion she'd given me to drink made my body sluggish. The slow floating met resistance and I pulled at it, struggling to get free of whatever I was snagged on. With a tug, I jerked upward and the next time I opened my eyes—

I was staring down at my body. There were gasps from my mates as I took in their shocked expressions. They must be able to see me because of the smoke. Nichelle's eyes had rolled to the back of her head as she chanted, power thrumming around her. As I watched, her eyes rolled back into focus, fixing on me. Filled with insanity. With a maniacal smile, she shrieked with laughter and clapped her hands once.

A whirlpool of wind closed around me, and I was hurled through the vortex—

—into a landscape that was as odd as it was familiar. The air shimmered with heat and the acrid scent of sulfur burned my nose.

Had she sent me to the right place? Was that part of her usual ritual, or had Nichelle indeed lost touch with reality right before she sent me here? I peered into the gloom, the shadows looming heavy and thick. A hiss slithered down from somewhere high above me and I craned my head just to see more shadows.

"Hello?" I asked. My voice was meek, even though I didn't intend it to be. Deep crevasses in the stone floor glowed with fire far below. The heat was oppressive.

Megiste, why are you here? You aren't ready. The voice sounded dismayed.

I turned in circles, but the shadows seemed to grow thicker. "I have questions."

You shouldn't be here.

"But I am. Please, talk to me."

There was silence, until thick globs of lava dropped from the ceiling, followed by a long, low, dangerous hiss.

The voice came again. *Look up.*

I froze. It felt like I was fighting through paralysis as I tried to lift my head, my eyes rolling upward. I stared into the dark to see a shape moving within it. Lines of fire ignited to form a pattern, outlining something large. A giant pair of wings unfurled, sending sparks raining over me, and I threw my arms over my head. Horror gripped me as a long sinewy neck extended toward me, the dragon's long snout and massive jaws fixing me with a toothy smile.

Run!

I took off like a shot, sprinting into the darkness, hands held up in front of me so I wouldn't run headlong into a wall.

The dragon roared and wind gusted through the cavern as it took flight in pursuit.

"Fuck!" I pushed my legs harder, trying to build speed. How the hell was I supposed to outrun a dragon?

I could only see a couple of feet ahead at any time, and my heart pounded as I realized there were vents and cracks in the floor that weren't illuminated by fire within them. If the dragon didn't get me, I'd die because I fell to my death in a dark pit. Or maybe I'd just impale myself tripping on a stalagmite.

Right after I thought about it, my fear came true as my foot caught on a ledge. I went sprawling to the ground with a whoosh of air pummeled from my lungs. How could it hurt so much when I didn't even have a physical body? The dragon advanced, long ropes of liquid fire oozing from its mouth.

Its head reared, and I closed my eyes, expecting at any moment to feel its jaws closing around me.

But they didn't. Instead, I heard a choking squelch. I risked a glance and saw the dragon, an invisible hand around its throat. A gurgling hiss escaped past the jagged teeth as its forked tongue tasted the air, swiping at its opponent but finding nothing to connect with.

Keep moving! I can't hold it for long.

I ran, feet chewing up the distance, as I headed for a faint glow up ahead. There was a small tunnel, and I darted into it, following its slight curve until I turned a corner and barely missed braining myself on a low cut of rock.

My feet slid on the gravel as I halted. I was in a vast chamber with a set of massive gates ahead of me. The iron glowed with a cold light, and I gagged at the stench.

Farah told me I needed to be dropped inside the gates. Judging by the chain with links that were bigger than my entire body, I was definitely *outside*.

The dragon roared, and the ground shook as it was freed from the grip of my savior. The vibrations backtracked the way it had chased me. It couldn't get through the small passage I'd run through, so it was going around.

I willed myself to return to my body. I'd have to try again, but at least I wouldn't get barbecued. Nothing happened. "Why can't I leave?"

The telltale poundings of the dragon's footsteps could no longer be heard, but the rush of wind told me everything I needed to know. It was flying, picking up speed. I didn't have minutes. It would be on me any second.

The fear of that thought brought something else out in me. I could feel magic twisting around me, and I embraced it. It shifted, almost like light reflecting on a crystal. I wasn't entirely sure what I was making it do, but when the dragon came into view, I braced myself. The dragon landed with a heavy thud, rearing up on its hind legs as it searched for me.

It didn't see me. It must be Felix's illusion magick that I was tapping into.

The dragon dropped down to all fours and sniffed the ground like a scent dog. I cursed. I didn't know if the illusion would hold up if it touched me.

I turned to the gate and wove my magick, bending my location into the space on the other side of the gate, exactly what I'd done to get Felix back.

A chorus of groans and wails slammed into my head, and I almost fell to my knees from the overwhelming force of it. Was this some kind of defense to keep me out?

Megiste—

The voice was barely audible over the cries and the dragon was getting closer. I pushed my magick harder, willing the two points to connect. The wailing grew louder, and I could feel the hot breath of the dragon as it got within a few feet of me.

The portal opened, and I jumped through to the other side, letting it snap shut just as a massive, clawed foot landed where I'd been standing.

What have you done?

The words were filled with heartbreak, and I realized the wails were echoing all around me now. It had been the Titans.

Chapter Ten

Bel

I hadn't specified a place for the portal to spit me out, so I wasn't too surprised when I found myself in the middle of a desert, nothing but sand stretching away for miles in any direction. I hopped between times, getting my distance from the Hounds, hoping they wouldn't have a way of tracking me.

Modern day Costa Rica, the Forbidden City, Tulum, prehistoric Siberia. Jumping from one place to the next, never staying more than a few minutes. I came to a stop somewhere in the middle of Nova Scotia, unsure of what year it was. Now the biggest question was whether I dared to go immediately to Legion. The Hounds weren't stupid, nor was Risha. They may have assumed that I would just take off to a time that I was comfortable with, but they also may have noticed my interest when they mentioned the chaos demon's name.

It wouldn't do me any harm to wait. On the contrary, out here in the middle of nowhere would be a great place to continue to recharge. I would bide my time. I would need to gain more of my strength back anyway if this plan were to work. Even diminished, Legion would prove powerful, and I'd only have one shot.

I continued to build up my power, changing locations periodically to ensure the Hounds didn't catch up with me. I'd been focusing on Paris, searching through different times in the construction of Notre-Dame. It was a safe bet it was relatively early in its lifespan, given that all the Desma were thrown into the past. Within a hundred years of its construction, I sensed Legion's presence. Now it was a matter of pinpointing when they were weakest.

Finally, on a cold, rainy day that blissfully tamped down the smell of shit in the streets, I found it. The cathedral was dark and empty. Its priest had mysteriously disappeared, and the diocese was in flux until the Vatican could sort things out with a new priest to take his place. The doors were still open to parishioners, so I decided it would be rude not to light a candle for the man.

Hopefully, they'd find a replacement that wasn't beholden to an ancient chaos demon.

The cellar was damp and I could smell Meg's mates. I spat in disgust. The wolf and the vampire. I was on the right track, then. The trapdoor squealed open, and I descended the stairs to find a large chamber lit with torches that were burning low over a scene of carnage. Legion's torn and bloodied bodies lay everywhere on grass stained black.

I walked among the corpses, admiring the work the Hounds had done. The shadows on the outer edges of the chamber writhed and slithered. A subtle glow next to the stone altar caught my attention, and I bent to pick up a large, flat stone that had the polish of cut glass. I studied the curious thing, and my eyes grew wide as I got an inkling of the magick it held. This would be even more beneficial than I thought.

"Why have you come, Belsioch?"

I turned to look at the pathetic creature that had spoken. There were two standing on opposite sides of the chamber. As I watched, two more appeared.

"Is this all that's left of you?" I asked.

Legion didn't answer with words, but several other bodies appeared from the inky darkness. They didn't last, though. The bodies flickered and warped, before winking out as if they'd never been there.

"Good show, old man," I said, tone mocking. There was nothing to fear from this being anymore.

"Are you going to kill me?" they asked.

My brow knit in confusion. "No. That would be a waste."

They stared, unblinking, and I continued.

"I would like to propose a solution to both our problems."

"There's nothing you could offer us," they said, turning to go back into the shadows.

I smirked. "Not even if I offered you vengeance?"

Legion paused and the individual bodies melted into one before they walked toward me a few paces. "Against the Hounds?"

I nodded, smiling at the gleam of hatred in their eyes. "Yes."

"How?"

"Possess me," I said, with as much casual indifference as if I was ordering coffee.

"What?"

"You heard me. You have my permission to enter my body. Make yourself at home. Use me as a vessel." I opened my arms wide.

"That's never been done. It could destroy us both."

I looked at them, incredulous. "I don't have much to lose anymore. Do you? Is your alchemist even alive?"

Legion hesitated, looking around at their empire which would soon decay without their magick sustaining it. "No. Vincent died when the Hounds destroyed most of my bodies. He was too deeply under my control."

"Shame. He sounded like a brilliant psychopathic mind."

"If we do this—"

"My offer expires in ten seconds," I said, holding out my hand.

Legion stared at it, their face impassive but their eyes raging. They nodded in a quick staccato and grasped my hand.

CHAPTER ELEVEN

Meg

I was in hell.

A literal, stinking, festering, horrible, putrefied, torturous nightmare.

I stared around me, the terrible realness of this place hitting me so hard I wanted to scream. To curl up in the fetal position and weep, hiding my eyes. Add my wails of despair to the cacophony of others.

Then the smell hit me. I collapsed and vomited until only bile came up, tears streaming down my face. My stomach continued to attempt its purge and cramped my muscles from the effort.

When I finally regained control of my body, I tried to stand. It took a couple of attempts, but I managed it. The cries had fallen silent, and I raised a trembling hand to wipe my mouth.

The gigantic scale of the chamber meant I couldn't see much at any one time, but what I did was more horrible than anything I could imagine. There was a path that led away through the rough terrain, making for easier travel to each of the—. I paused. Tortures. The individual tortures each Titan was being subjected to.

I'd underestimated how truly giant these beings were. The stories didn't do them justice. I didn't know them by sight, but I could guess from the tortures they'd been given, who they were. Helios was torched by the sun, Atlas was being crushed, Rhea eaten alive by her own garden, Oceanus deprived of the element he loved most.

Pallas was being forced to fight against the weakest enemies and as I passed, he was slain. Prometheus was smoldering, being immolated by the fire he'd gifted humanity with. Theia had her eyes put out, surrounded by a brilliant sky she would never see again.

Each of them turned their faces as I passed, pain and anguish etched on their features. I was sobbing uncontrollably by the time I reached the highest point on the path. Kronos crawled in filth, broken crowns puncturing his hands and knees.

A cry tore from my throat as I fell, collapsing into a heap. "This is what he's done to you?"

Kronos didn't answer, didn't stop crawling. I folded in on myself, burying my face in my hands. Bel was a monster, but this? This was a level of depravity I couldn't fathom, even though the evidence was right in front of me. It shattered my mind to pieces, imagining what they'd been suffering for thousands of years.

"Megiste." His deep voice boomed, and I startled, leaping to my feet.

I looked up. Kronos hadn't stopped moving, but as he passed me, he turned and caught my eye. There were so many emotions there, I couldn't discern any one.

"Why did you go through the gate?"

My face scrunched in confusion. "The dragon—"

He shook his head, his mane of long, shaggy hair getting trampled as he moved, caked in muck. "You were hidden from it. Why did you go through?"

"It would've found me, I—wait. Did something happen when I went through it?"

Kronos waited until he could turn his head back to me to speak. He was looking at me like a father scolding his child for being a fool, but his tone wasn't quite so harsh. "You imprinted your signature on it. If Belsioch discovers this, he'll be able to lock you out."

"What?" My heart crashed into my stomach. "I didn't know. Nichelle was supposed to drop me on this side of them, but she miscalculated." Or had she? "It doesn't change anything. I'm not giving up, even if Bel figures it out."

My hair moved as Kronos let out a breath. "I admire your faith. But it is not that simple. Especially not now that you only have five of your protectors."

I shook my head. "Wait. That's the reason I'm here. There is so much I—*we*, don't know. Farah told me to come here to get more information, so we didn't fail. We have no plan. And if you had one, you didn't share it with the class."

My anger was getting the better of me. Don't discipline me like I misbehaved when you didn't even explain the rules. "I can only do so much with the information I was given."

There was a long silence, and I squirmed. "You are right," said Kronos. "But that doesn't change what's happened."

I cocked my head in annoyance. "So explain the plan to me, and we'll go from there. How did you all plan for this to go down?"

Another excruciating pause. "You were all to journey down here. The path is long and dark, and you will need to rely on each other. The challenges you will face will require the various powers of your mates. But already that will become an almost insurmountable task since you no longer have Arthur." He took a shuddering breath, the wet squelch of his movements filling the silence.

"You are the key. The magick woven into those doors prevents us from touching them. It would kill us on contact. The signatures of every one of our brethren who died are woven into it, used against us. You were supposed to infuse the gate with our signatures, which we gave you when we created you. It would undo the binding and turn it in our favor. We could leave this place. But now that you've put *your* signature on the gate... if you touch it again, you'll seal it forever. We won't have another chance at escape."

"No," I whispered. Was Nichelle working with Bel, or did she just do this out of revenge? Did she even know what she'd done?

"How do I fix it?" I asked. "There has to be a way to fix it."

Kronos didn't answer, but I could see tears in his eyes.

My soul tugged at me, wanting to return to its body. "I'm not giving up," I said. "I will find a way to fix this."

And then I opened my eyes to my mates staring down at me. I was still crying. Nichelle watched us with a crazed grin. "What did you do?" I screamed, launching at her. I knocked her back and pinned her to the floor, but instead of fighting back, she only laughed.

Her laughter became a shriek as she stared into space, clawing at her face before devolving into soft chuckles. The madness had taken her again.

"What's happening?" Andrus asked, pulling me off her.

I ran a hand over my face, trying to fight back tears and failing. "I might've just doomed the Titans."

Gareth volunteered to run back to the nearest town and find a phone to call a ride. He was confident Time would help him figure it out, and I let him. By the time I'd finished telling them what had happened, I was barely intelligible I was crying so hard.

Nichelle was still giggling to herself in the corner.

"Do you think Farah was in on it?" asked Felix.

Andrus was wrapped around me, trying to share every ounce of comfort and calm he could.

"No," I answered, voice quavering.

Felix gave me a doubtful look. "Meg, maybe—"

"No!" I sucked in a breath. "Nichelle had one of her episodes at the worst possible time and either someone influenced her to do what she did, or she did it as a way to get even with me."

"Sabotaging our chances at freeing the Titans seems a bit out of balance with stealing a grimoire," said Remi.

"Does she look like she's thinking clearly, right now?" asked Felix, aiming a glare at Nichelle. "We shouldn't have let you do this. I knew it was a bad idea."

"Don't start. It's your job to protect me, not control me," I snapped. "You don't *let* me do anything. I'm not your charge,

I'm your mate! An equal! Start acting like it!" My only regret as my ire rose was that Gareth had run to town and wasn't here to share in the tongue lashing.

"I'm sorry, I didn't mean to—"

"Like hell you didn't, Felix!" I jumped to my feet, tearing off my clothes and heading for the door.

"Meg, wait!" said Andrus, but I was already gone.

I raced through the trees, my wolf overjoyed at being loosed.

"Meg!" Andrus was running after me, gaining ground. I tore off the road and into the swamp, trying to find a solid path through and hoping I could lose him.

I fought the urge to howl, but the ache sat heavy in my chest. Why couldn't anything go right? I just needed to get away. The howl tore free, filled with all the pain and anguish of yet another failure, possibly a catastrophic one this time. What if we couldn't recover from this?

When the sounds of pursuit faded, I slowed. Finding a patch of land that seemed relatively safe to rest on, I curled up on the boggy earth. The sounds of the swamp invaded my thoughts, and I let them lull me with their hypnotic song.

"Let's take a walk. That gator is eyeing you for a meal."

I looked up to find a tall man with a muscular build and bright eyes standing over me. Straight brown hair fell to his shoulders, and there was a small gap in his front teeth when he fixed me with a tired smile.

I blew air out my nose and shook my head.

Death's face was kind, and he motioned for me to follow anyway. I got to my feet, keeping my wolf form, and followed.

"So things went a bit sideways, huh?"

I yipped.

"I'm not going to say it'll be easy to surpass this, but don't give up all hope just yet."

My sad whine cut through the air.

He shrugged. "Nobody said this job would be easy. But you accepted the challenge. Are you really going to back down now?"

I stopped, and he waited as I changed back. He conjured a long coat from thin air and offered it to me, which I gratefully accepted.

"I have no intentions of backing down. Things just get so overwhelming, and now this latest setback..." I felt helpless. "Can't somebody just give me a fucking guidebook? Why does everyone seem to hold back pivotal information that could prevent catastrophe?"

Death chuckled. "It's not intentional. Most of the time anyway." He took a breath. "You have to understand that when you've been around as long as we have, we start to take things for granted. Things we've always known, that we think are common knowledge. Even esoteric magickal practices that no one has used in thousands of years. It was all the rage when we learned about it. And I'm willing to bet the Titans are just as furious at themselves for failing to realize that. All of their carefully laid plans are in jeopardy because of an oversight this minimal."

"Was Farah working against me?"

"No. You were correct in your assumption about Nichelle. She's not well."

We walked a little longer and I could see the main road ahead of us. All my mates were waiting, Gareth included.

"How do we fix this?" I asked.

"I'm assuming they told you about Arthur," said Death, cutting right to the point.

"A little," I said. "Just that his absence would make the journey to Tartarus harder."

"We can start there, then."

I blinked. "Can you bring him back?"

He laughed heartily. "No. Well," he paused, flopping his hand back and forth. "I mean, I could, but I won't. This is Hades's territory we're talking about. No way, no how, am I going anywhere near it. He and I haven't seen eye to eye for quite a while."

"How many Ætherim do you have beef with?" I asked.

"That list is too long to count." He rolled his eyes. "What I can do is get you into Hades's lands without being detected. After that, you're on your own. And I highly suggest you do not get caught."

"Hades would be the least of my problems. Most of my foster family is dead, but they had a lot of allies. I haven't been back there since Bel—" I couldn't even finish the sentence. Bile still rose in my throat every time I thought about what a hero I'd turned Bel into. The savior I'd allowed him to become.

"Don't waste any time being concerned about them. The threat they pose is minimal. They might give you a small spot of trouble, but you can handle yourself. But if Hades finds you... he's not been himself for centuries."

"How so?"

Death was quiet, lost in thought. I almost walked away to give him time to himself. "The Ætherim have been fading. It's natural in the cycle of any immortal being. Being alive for so long wears on the mind. Most of us don't catch it until it's too late. By the time we realize we've changed, we're comfortable with who we've become. He is no exception."

"Wait. Is that why Bel—"

Death appraised me, as if trying to decide what to tell me. "Bel has changed significantly. His heart used to be in the right place."

I opened my mouth to ask more questions, but Death held up his hand. "It's not important. He is now the biggest threat that we are facing. That is the key thing to focus on."

"But—"

"I will not be discussing that further with you. But you can take it as a warning. Look at Bel's behavior and keep that in mind as you try to avoid running into the lord of the underworld at all costs. Bel's madness is on the surface. Hades's runs deep. He's always been... cantankerous. But that has become a seething anger over the centuries, and he delivers his madness with a smile while throwing his elaborate parties."

I stared, confused. I've been to some real ragers thrown by older Ætherim families, and they put a whole new level on the meaning of lecherousness, but I've never seen anything that would be cause for outright fear.

He knew what I was thinking. "Don't test the theory. If you are found, I won't be able to help you. You'll have to find your own way out. And if you wind up in his Halls, stay away from the lower floors. Once he has you down there, escaping Tartarus will seem easy."

"We've faced a lot of things and come out just fine on the other end," I said, motioning to the men behind us.

Death shook his head. "They will not be going with you."

I gaped. "Why the hell not?"

"You spent enough time there, you know the answer."

"But they shouldn't be at risk for that. Not with our bonding. And if it's a short enough time, it wouldn't be an issue anyway."

"It never ceases to amaze me how little you know. Those idiots who raised you should be ashamed of themselves."

"They never knew the definition of shame," I muttered.

"Being bonded with you will give them a small amount of protection against becoming shades in the underworld, but it will not save them from that place leaving its mark on them. It will be a pull, trying to draw them back in every chance it gets."

I paused. Of course I knew about that issue, but I grew up there and never had a problem. And there have been others that have been there and escaped, and not had much worse to deal with.

"If you have a strong enough anchor holding you here, it's not that much of a risk." I tried to say it with more confidence than I felt in the fact.

Death stroked his chin. "Yes, to a point. But besides that, moving you into that realm without being detected will be hard enough without four others accompanying you. I have no chance of keeping you hidden if they go with you. And then Hades, or any of his minions, will be on you in a second. He's already salty that someone escaped him twice. Interlopers do not go unnoticed for long."

"Who would be dumb enough to go back there if they'd already escaped the underworld once?"

"It wasn't her choice," he said casually, but I could tell from his tone of voice that there was much more to the story. "At some point you may meet. You can ask her yourself."

The glint of mischief in his eyes was intriguing, and it didn't get by me how fond he sounded of her.

"Even given those risks, I doubt I'll be able to convince them to stay behind."

"There will be no convincing needed," he said, all trace of affection disappearing. "They will have a task of their own to worry about. Given by me, so they can't delay. This will be a journey for you, and you alone."

There was such an intensity in his gaze. No matter how much I wanted to call it out for hyperbole, I knew he was telling me the truth. But if this mission was so dangerous, how was there any hope of being able to find Arthur without being detected by the king of the realm? When unusual things happen, like a random living person appearing out of nowhere, waltzing around the planes of the dead, life energy lit up like a beacon, it gets noticed. And even if all of that went according to plan...

"What happens if I do find Arthur? Won't all of his memories be gone?"

"Quite possibly, but there are workarounds, not the least of which is that fancy new trick of yours. Bending timelines and joining two different versions of a person together? Very clever."

"I can't take credit for that one, it was all Gareth."

Death shot Gareth a look as he stood with the rest of my mates, staring after us, ready to act if needed. "I wonder if it's anything to do with him being your first bonded mate." He said it more to himself than to me. "Or maybe Time already took a liking to him." He shook his head.

"I must go. You have two days, while I get clarification on a few things. And then It's off to the underworld with you."

Chapter Twelve

Remi

After we'd returned to Farah's house, Meg disappeared into the private library and we hadn't seen her all day. Now evening was rolling around again.

"We should go in there," said Andrus. "I'm sure Farah will understand."

"Are you kidding? She almost ripped our heads off once when we told her what happened. And I think she's in there with Meg," said Felix.

"I'll go," I said.

They turned to look at me. "Farah hates you enough already," said Felix.

I shrugged. "So be it. I'll take the risk."

"We're already planning an excursion to the underworld to retrieve one of our fallen. Let's not make it a double," said Andrus.

I waited until they went back to their debate before I slipped away down the stairs. The library doors swung open silently. I closed them behind me and headed toward soft voices in the back.

"I wish I had better answers for you, or words of comfort," said Farah. "The last time I spoke to Nichelle she was doing so much better. The problems this caused may not have a solution."

Meg said something I couldn't hear.

Farah sighed. "I am sorry for not warning you ahead of time what you might find there. But I think it's better for you to have seen it. Now you know what you're fighting for."

"We'll find something. If there's not a fix for it, we invent one. It's magick. Nothing is true and anything is possible. You just have to figure out how to make it happen." Meg sniffed. "I just hope we all make it out of this and have a chance to really figure out what kind of family we are. What if Bel did too much of a number on my head and I destroy these relationships, even if I don't want to? And we're bound together, so what happens then? We just live with each other until we snap and turn on the others?"

"How long have you been holding onto these fears?"

"These ones are pretty new."

Farah chuckled softly. "You have every right to feel what you're feeling, but I also have a right to tell you that you're full of shit and worrying for nothing."

"Wow," said Meg.

"This is a sign of a healthy relationship, dear. That's why you don't recognize it. You're all comfortable enough to speak your minds. With personalities as strong as you all have, there will be trouble. Can you imagine if they played follow the leader and never asked questions? That would be a much bigger problem."

"I suppose you're right," said Meg.

"Of course I am." There was a pause. "I have a meeting to get to."

"Okay. Thank you for listening to my rants."

"Anytime."

Footsteps moved past me in the aisle to my right. I waited until I was sure Farah was gone, and then I stepped into the open.

"Meg."

She jumped, the book she'd just picked up falling to the floor. She gave me a small smile. "Of course you're the one that ignores Farah's warning to keep out." I retrieved her book and handed it to her, and she motioned to the chair across from her. I took a seat. "How much of that conversation did you hear?"

I shrugged. "Not much. The last couple of minutes."

"Now you know more of my dirty little insecurities," she joked, but there was sadness in her eyes.

"I know things got ugly out there, but we're worried about you," I said gently.

She took a deep breath, and I thought she was going to tell me to leave.

"Have you ever wanted something so badly, and were so afraid to admit it that when the chance to have that thing comes along, all you do is try to sabotage it?"

I raised an eyebrow. "That's my entire life in a nutshell."

She snorted. "Yeah, I guess it is."

"What in particular are you sabotaging? Because it's not the relationship you have with us."

Her lips parted and she cast her eyes down. "It sure feels like it. I'm having attention lavished on me by several wonderful men, I finally have a shot at the family I've always wanted, and yet the more the reality of it sinks in, the less comfortable I become with it. And every new mate only adds to the stress. It has to be too good to be true."

"You can't let your fear overtake you. Maybe this entire group is still in its honeymoon phase—"

She barked a laugh. "This is you in the honeymoon phase? Good gods."

I chucked. "I apologize for nothing." I leaned back and kicked my feet up on the small table in front of me.

Meg's eyes danced with humor, but she said nothing about the scuff marks I was sure to leave on Farah's table.

"If there's one thing I've learned, it's to never take your family for granted. Enjoy every day you have with them, even when things are troubled. There's plenty of time to second guess everything when they're gone."

"Speaking from experience?" she asked.

I debated. Part of me wanted to tell her. She'd understand, and I'd been carrying this burden for so long. But if she judged me harshly, which I would deserve...

"I only told you a small portion of how I came to be in that dungeon." The stumps of my wings twinged with pain at the very mention. Dread roiled in my gut, but I pushed it away.

"When I arrived in Paris, they'd only just begun laying the foundation of the cathedral. As you can imagine, I took a liking to the height of the building. I hadn't yet met my wife when things started to take a turn at Notre-Dame."

Meg made a sound of surprise. "Wife?"

"Yes. Mona." Unbidden, her face appeared in my mind's eye. The delicate brown curls that always fell into her face, no matter how hard she tried to keep them under control. The small gap in her front teeth when she smiled her soft, glowing smile that erased every pain. Bright blue eyes that saw right through my hard, rocky armor and loved me no matter what form I took.

The empty gaze as she stared into the sky, waiting for me to swoop down and save her, blood mixing with the freckles that dusted her face. But I wasn't there. I didn't save her. I pressed my hands to my eyes on the pretense of clearing dust, wanting desperately to wipe away the memory.

"She was human. I had recently entered King Charles's court and was rising in the ranks. She was one of the queen's ladies. We tried to hide our relationship for both our sakes, but as I continued to earn more of the king's favor and not a little from the queen as well, I decided to make a request."

"That they allow you to marry Mona."

"Yes," I said, barely a whisper. "I funded a great deal of the cathedral architecture, always wanting them to build higher." I smiled ruefully. "They took it as a sign of my egotism. They still didn't turn down my money, but I knew I was the butt of many a joke. I didn't care. I just wanted a place to land and observe the city." I chuckled. "It was truly peaceful. And as it grew, I had a young family that was growing too."

"Children?" she asked.

"Three daughters."

A different pain struck me as I remembered them running to me every time I came home, their tiny hands reaching, begging to be picked up and spun around. Angels in human form. A shuddering breath racked my lungs at the lancing agony, my heart constricting.

Meg was on her feet and kneeling next to me in an instant, taking my hand and peering into my face. She said nothing, her comforting presence enough. I smiled at her, grateful, and squeezed her hand.

I glanced out the window and noticed the gathering storm clouds. A walk in the rain sounded like a great idea. "Would you like to go outside? Walk and talk?" I asked.

She didn't seem as enthusiastic about getting rained on, but she agreed. We snuck out so the others wouldn't try to follow. The streets weren't as busy this far from the entertainment district, so we could walk side by side without being jostled constantly as people pushed past.

A rumble of thunder pealed in the distance and I smiled. "I've always loved rain. It's one thing I missed the most in that dungeon."

Meg nodded. "Thunderstorms are my favorite. The noise is always comforting."

The evening was perfect, the gas lamps lit in the fading sunset making for a picturesque stroll as the storm rolled in.

I continued my story. "I didn't know the infiltration was Legion, but I could feel something wasn't right. And it wasn't in my nature to sit things out and see what happened. So I took it upon myself to act as guardian. A sense of dread had been building around Notre-Dame for years and it felt like whatever was there was ready to make its move. I had just received the title of Marquise and gave so much money for the construction of the cathedral, I basically was given free rein to wander the place. Even the private quarters. Nobody batted an eye."

Thunder rumbled closer, and the raindrops pattered lightly on the sidewalk.

"So when I went looking deeper into the foundations, nobody thought it strange either. I'm assuming Gareth and Andrus found the cellar entrance when they went snooping?"

Meg nodded. "I still can't believe that entire setup was beneath the cathedral."

"Legion had turned it into one big siphon. Growing fat off the hope and wonder and reverence of the people. To possess the entire city. And sink their claws deep into a few special souls."

We turned down a street with a thick canopy of trees lining it. The rain fell a little harder, the canopy shielding us and providing a musical backdrop of droplets falling through the leaves. I took a moment to settle my nerves.

I glanced at Meg. She was staring ahead, but when she noticed I'd gone silent, she looked at me.

She smiled shyly. "What?"

When I slipped my fingers between hers, I thought for sure she'd pull away. Her small hand fit into mine perfectly and I allowed myself a moment to enjoy it.

I was still trying to figure her out. She'd cast a spell on me from the moment I'd set eyes on her. I'd unleashed every bit of hardness and cruelty I had to push her away and get her to leave me in that dungeon to suffer as I deserved to suffer. She refused. Even gave some of it right back.

Maybe there was some magick that was drawing us together, but the influence ended there. Things felt natural with her. There was an instant ease she brought with her that soothed me when nothing and no one had ever been able to.

She felt like home.

I'd grieved so many losses, and thought I'd hardened myself to all but the deaths of my wife and children. But, even though I had a terrible way of showing it, the idea of losing her too was like reopening that wound. I couldn't leave her or the others now, even if I tried. She'd even rekindled my faith in the mission we'd been set. Despite the setbacks we'd just suffered, I somehow knew that we'd still find a way. The Titans were wise beyond all measure, but even they could overlook things.

The lights on tall iron posts were quite beautiful, flickering with flame, each one along this street complete with landscaping around it. Night-blooming flowers. There were two things about this modern world that I'd determined; it was loud and overly stimulating, and yet it was capable of simple beauty. Small things that you might have to look hard for sometimes, but they were there. You could step outside the hectic nature of humankind and all its distractions for a simple moment, such as a fragrant bloom or the perfect placement of a cat sitting on a brick wall backlit by the moon. To connect with a part of you that you'd forgotten was there.

Or the feeling of fingers twined with your own as you walked down a quiet street in the rain.

"I came upon Legion in that underground chamber and we fought. I don't know what I was thinking. It had been a couple thousand years since I'd battled anything stronger than an ogre. Even though I didn't know the creature for Legion at the time, I knew it was terribly powerful. And I went after it anyway."

I tilted my face toward the rain. So much blood and pain. They'd broken me across their knee like I was nothing. Left me in a heap to die.

"Of course, Legion figured out who I was. A prominent figure in court doesn't go unnoticed. Legion's puppets told the king what I was. They stripped me of my title, secretly, all protections and privileges removed. I was too well-liked by the people to just make me disappear, so they spread the word that I'd fallen ill." My jaw clenched as I fought the lump in my throat. "And they went after my family. Legion allowed me to leave the chamber. I was of no consequence to them. I'm not sure how long it took me to recover enough that I escaped, but it was too late. I arrived back home to find my family slain, left hanging in the front hall."

My shoulders shook as I fought back the anguish. The rain poured down on us now, but Meg made no move to hurry us along. She brought us to a halt and wrapped her arms around my middle. The top of her head barely reached my chest. I held her close, a lifeline.

"As I cut the bodies down and laid them alongside each other, the king's guard arrived. They watched me dig the graves of my wife and children before arresting me. I didn't resist. It was my penance. For failing them."

Meg tilted her head and gazed at me, her eyes so full of compassion it only made my pain worse. "So now you know the truth. And how I failed. You shouldn't let me stay." I said the words, heart breaking, but knowing it would be best if she agreed. Damn, but I hoped to the Fates that she wouldn't.

"Remi."

I blinked. Her tone was... reproachful. She placed her hands on my cheeks, thumbs skimming along the ridges of my cheekbones.

"Why would you think I'd make you leave?"

My voice was thick with emotion. "Because I couldn't protect them. I've already jeopardized *us* by not taking my wings back when I had the chance. There's no reason I won't fail all of you, too."

Her brow furrowed, and she looked off to the side, shaking her head. This was it. She was about to cast me out.

"You can be really stupid sometimes," she said. She pulled my face down to hers and kissed my forehead before resting her own against mine. Her fingers played with the hairs at my nape while her other continued to cup my cheek. "You're not going anywhere. You belong with us. And whatever happened in the past, is past. You were alone then. You won't be alone anymore."

Like a dam breaking, I was overcome. I sank to my knees and buried my face in her stomach, clinging to her. A sob tore from me, and she held me while I felt everything. It was a catharsis I'd never allowed myself.

When I stood again, it was like a weight had been lifted. Meg shared my pain that day, freeing me from some of the guilt. I would never, *could* never forgive myself, but she was right. I wasn't alone in this anymore.

As we approached the front door of Farah's house, it opened to reveal the other three waiting for us.

CHAPTER THIRTEEN

Meg

We stood in the foyer, dripping rainwater all over Farah's carpet runner. I hadn't brought the other three in on me and Remi's talk. It felt too much like a violation of trust. But there were certain things I'd never be able to hide, strong emotional reactions being one. They put the pieces together from the snippets that broke through whenever I was so shocked or horrified by what he'd said that my flimsy privacy walls tumbled.

The three men stood, looking at Remi with fresh eyes.

"I'm sorry," said Gareth. "I was a jackass. I didn't think—"

Remi shook his head. "I would've reacted the same if our roles were reversed."

Gareth stepped forward and pulled Remi into a hug, the wet slaps of his hand on Remi's drenched shirt loud in the entryway. Andrus and Felix repeated the gesture, welcoming their brother back into the fold.

I took a few steps toward the stairs, my shoes squishing as I did so. I winced. "Farah's gonna be so mad."

"Correct," said a firm voice. Farah was leaning against the doorframe, watching us. "Go get cleaned up. And next time you take a walk in the rain, use the back stairs."

I regretted not buying a backup set of comfortable clothing as I peeled out of the drenched fabric, tossing it in the tub. All I had left that was decently clean was the chemise that I wore underneath the party dress from last night. All the other clothing that Farah had been keeping up here had disappeared for some reason.

I wrung out my clothes and went in search of the dryer while Remi took his turn to clean up. My hunt was successful, and I was about to head upstairs when I heard familiar voices in the kitchen.

"Woah. Farah's staff let you in here?" I asked, finding Gareth, Andrus, and Felix gathered around the kitchen island, snacking on a plate of finger foods and sandwiches that had been left out. "I hope to the gods that those weren't meant for something else."

"It's quite alright, miss," said an older man. He was dressed like a chef, so I supposed this was his domain. "I thought y'all might be hungry and dinner won't be for a few hours yet."

"Thank you..." I said.

"Peter," the man replied.

"Peter." My stomach growled, and I laughed. "Clearly, your instincts were correct."

"Not at all," he said, waving away the compliment. "Now if you'll excuse me, I need to run to the market. Make yourselves at home." He grabbed a large, empty tote bag and slung it over his shoulder on the way out the door. I gave a small wave before turning back to the feast. I was relieved both that I had food in front of me and that I wouldn't be scraping my mates off the walls when Farah discovered they'd eaten the snacks for a tea she was hosting, or whatever she was up to today.

It seemed to be an unspoken agreement that we wouldn't discuss Remi's confession. So I told them about my discussion with Death instead.

"Where do you think he intends to send us?" asked Andrus.

"I'm more concerned about the fact that he expects you to go to the underworld alone," said Gareth.

"I was wondering," said Felix. "Since it was you four that made the deal with him, are the rest of us exempt? After this is over, can we just agree to disagree and not participate in whatever he had planned?"

I shifted uneasily. Gareth and Andrus shared the concern I felt about Felix's casual attitude toward our group.

The wolf growled. "Are you implying you have no intention of staying?"

Felix shook his head. "No. But I didn't agree to this bargain or whatever you want to call it. I don't like the idea that you've signed me up for something and I have no idea what I'm in for."

Gareth took a step forward, but I stopped him with a hand firmly on his chest.

"That's fine," I said to Felix. "You can talk to Death yourself. It'll make things a bit... awkward... if you choose not to continue. But it's your choice."

"Thank you. At least someone is reasonable." He slapped my ass and things happened in a blur after that. Gareth lunged for him, Andrus a step behind, but neither touched him before Felix was pinned to the wall by his throat.

He choked, my hand clamping down tighter, claws extended. My thumb dug into his skin and a trickle of blood dripped down his neck. My tone was hard. "Why don't you just call me 'sugar tits' while you're at it."

I released him and Felix took in a shuddering breath.

"This is just a continuation of last night," I said, voice hard. "You don't listen."

"Meg—"

I pointed a finger in his face. "No. Let me repeat this. I really hope you're listening because I'm not saying it again. You are not my keeper. I am not an object. You will not treat me with such disrespect. If you want to go your own way after this is over, fine. I won't stop you. Hell, if you wanted to bounce right now..." I held my arms open. "Be my guest."

"Meg," said Andrus.

I turned to him and shared a look before returning my attention to Felix. "I'm giving him a chance to prove that he only cares about himself. Go ahead. Walk out that door. While the rest of the Six gravitated toward places where they could do the most good, you found yourself in a Roman vacation spot, indulging every desire you ever had. And when it was about to disappear, you planned to go with it rather than give up your life of luxury."

I took a step closer to him, his face ashen. "That's the real truth, isn't it? I'm sure you're a fantastic warrior. You clearly impressed the Titans enough to join their team, and I'm sure you did put your heart into the work." Our noses were almost touching. "But be honest with me. Did you do it all for the fame and glory? For the perks? For the money and riches and women?" I stepped back to stand beside Gareth. "Because if that's the case, you can fuck right off. We already have to regroup, so we'll do it without you."

His mouth worked like a fish until it snapped shut and he blew past me, out the back door.

"Uh. I'm not going to say that wasn't warranted, but..." said Andrus. "What if he actually leaves?"

I was so mad I was shaking, and Gareth put his hand on my shoulder. "Then we figure it out. She read him perfectly, 'drus. She called him out for what he is."

Remi entered the room. "Is that why he just rushed out the door?"

I turned and froze, clapping my hand to my mouth as I tried not to laugh. "Oh, no."

Andrus snorted, and Gareth stared wide eyed. Remi had grabbed a set of sweats to change into, but these were about five sizes too small.

The sweatpants had become capris that were doing their best to hold together as they stretched around his muscular thighs. The t-shirt struggled to accommodate his shoulders and chest and the arms looked like cap sleeves now, so tight I wondered if his circulation was being cut off.

"I'm glad this amuses you." He tried to put some growling aggravation into his voice, but the appearance of his dimples told another story. "All the damn dressers were empty. This was all I could find."

Farah passed by at just that moment, eyes sparkling. "Stay out of my library."

The sphinx walked away, and I couldn't contain my laughter.

"Thanks for taking the hit for us," said Gareth, between gulps of air.

Andrus had tears in his eyes, using the island for support. Remi just shook his head, a small smile on his face as he allowed himself to be the unwitting comic relief.

The mood lightened considerably after that.

Felix still wasn't home by the time we all sat down for dinner—Farah returned Remi's good clothes—and I was wondering if I'd made a mistake. I didn't regret calling Felix out for being an asshole. Just because we had a heart-to-heart about Arthur didn't mean he wasn't a misogynist. But I went overboard with my reaction.

I hoped he would come back so I could apologize.

"You wounded his pride. It will take him time to come to terms with that," said Farah. "But you gave him plenty of food for thought."

"He'll be eating leftovers of that meal for a month," said Andrus, shaking his head. "I thought for sure he'd come around. Once he saw what it was like to be bonded. He's never had a connection like that before."

"And it scares the piss out of me."

We all turned to see Felix standing in the entryway of the dining room.

"Can we talk?" he asked me.

"Go ahead," said Remi, eyeing him with annoyance.

"Please?" Felix said, nodding his head behind him.

I followed him into the hallway, and he walked with me out of earshot, more out of habit than anything.

"I was an ass," he began. When I didn't refute him, he continued. "You weren't wrong. About why I liked playing the hero. And I loved that lifestyle. Herculaneum was a perfect match for me. I'm a selfish prick."

He rubbed the back of his head. "Gods, this is hard." He sighed. "I think what I'm trying to say is—"

I held up my hand. "If you're about to say something about how you're scared of the bond and the feelings it's causing you to have, I'll know if you're lying."

Felix fell silent and I consider him, leaning against the wall. "It's a big change. I get it. But if you plan on staying—"

"I am," he said quickly. "Staying."

I nodded and took a breath. "I know it's for their sake, and that's okay. You have your loyalties and none of them lie with me."

He opened his mouth to protest, but I stopped him.

"Our relationship can be like a coworkers with benefits scenario. I'm fine with keeping things casual."

His mouth fell open. "Why are you being so accommodating? You were ready to rip my head off earlier."

"Because I was reacting in the moment, for which I'm sorry. People don't change just because you wish they would." He winced. "But I won't take it personally." I paused. "Even though you need to stop with that machismo bullshit."

Felix nodded, relief flooding the bond. As we headed back to the dining room, I said over my shoulder, "I can't guarantee Gareth and Andrus will feel the same."

They did not. Dinner ended quickly before the argument spilled over into violence. Night fell, and I was sitting on the balcony overlooking the gardens with Andrus and Remi. Andrus had slowly been pulling me closer over the last hour on the loveseat we shared, but I'd just repositioned myself in his lap entirely.

Gareth had gone down to prowl in his wolf form through the hedge maze, and a frustrated howl rose up every now and again. Felix was in the living room, keeping to himself and giving my mates time to cool down.

It was hot and humid, even in this extra little pocket of space that Farah had carved out of the universe, so I didn't change my clothes after they came out of the dryer, opting to stay in the thin chemise.

"Where do you think we are? In the cosmos?" I asked, staring up at the stars.

Andrus looked skyward and noticed the same thing I did. "Oh."

None of the constellations looked familiar.

"Did Farah create this herself?" asked Remi.

I pulled a face. "She's very secretive about using her magick, so I've never known just what she's capable of."

"Are you nervous about finding Arthur?" Andrus asked.

I rested my head on his shoulder. "I haven't thought about it much. The idea of going home makes me queasy. But I would like to have a chance to make things right with him."

Andrus leaned in for a kiss. "It will all be fine. You'll find him, we'll track down Hadi, and we'll break the Titans out of jail."

My hand was traveling along his thigh, aimless. "If only it were that simple."

"It doesn't have to be hard."

"Of course it does," I said.

Remi snorted, and I realized the double entendre. I looked at my mate and my hand paused on his upper thigh.

Andrus spoke against the shell of my ear. "If you want it hard, fated one, I can do that."

Shivers went down my spine, instantly igniting a fire within me. My hand moved the rest of the way to his cock, and I pulled Andrus's face to mine. "Please."

Our lips locked, tongues tangling. I didn't waste time straddling him, hands running over his chest. I was already fumbling with the drawstrings on his pants when a shadow loomed over me. Remi.

He kneeled down next to me, eyes searching mine. With incredible gentleness, he leaned in and kissed me, hands cupping my face. A whole new side of the gruff gargoyle appeared as he placed tender trails of kisses down my neck, leaving me breathless and wanting more.

Remi sat back on his heels and I leaned after him, still under his spell, before I caught myself. I blinked. "Does this mean you're ready?" I asked, licking my lips.

A genuine smile lit up his face to reveal the man he'd been hiding, the one trapped by the anguished memories. His next kiss was fevered and Andrus's hands moved up and down my body as I twined my fingers in Remi's hair. Footsteps announced Gareth's arrival and the heat coming off him as the arousal coursed through our bond was immense.

I took a quick glance and noticed Felix standing off to the side, looking uncomfortable. Everything came to a halt as we all turned to look at him.

Gareth growled. "I suppose he has to take part?"

My voice was careful, relaxed. "It's the only way Remi can bond with us. I'm okay with this, but are all of you?"

A heavy silence pervaded as they looked between each other, glaring at Felix. For his part, he didn't back down, but he was clearly nervous.

"Look," he said. "I can leave these pants on and just pull my cock out of the hole, if that makes you feel better."

"That won't be necessary," said Gareth, shaking his head with a light chuckle.

"Alright, then." I smiled. "Have at me."

Andrus claimed my lips while Remi tugged my chemise over my head. I tugged at Andrus's pants while he fumbled to get his shirt off, eventually ripping it. Clothing was soon scattered all over the balcony—except for Gareth, who hadn't bothered to put his back on after he'd run up here from the garden.

I gripped Andrus's cock and guided it to my entrance, sinking onto him without pause until I had him fully inside me. Andrus groaned, grabbing my hips and rocking into me as Remi kissed me with renewed fervor.

My vampire lifted my wrist to his mouth as his thrusts deepened. I bucked my hips against him and when he sank his teeth into my skin, I cried out. The magick of the bond rolled over us as the now familiar rainbow swirled in my eyes.

I ground down hard, chasing my ecstasy, my climax reaching its height when Andrus came, pulling his mouth from my wrist as he groaned, tipping his head back and emptying himself with a few small thrusts.

I pulled away from Remi and took Andrus's face in my hands, kissing him and tasting my blood. His hands ran over my breasts, and I arched my back as he moved one hand between my thighs to rub me. I rode him, looking for more friction, and his cock twitched back to life inside me. Before we could go for round two, Gareth was there.

My hips switched slowly, giving Andrus time, while I stroked Gareth before leaning over and licking his tip. His breath hitched, and I closed my mouth around him, running my tongue over his shaft, taking him deeper, an inch at a time. I was almost at the base of his cock when Andrus was ready to go.

He thrust upward, and I moaned around Gareth. Remi's hands joined, stroking my breasts while I was caught between my other two mates, helpless against the pleasure.

I gave up on trying to find a rhythm when my mind clouded under the haze of hands, lips and powerful thrusts, giving myself over to them completely. With every successive mate added to our group, this part of the ritual became more all-consuming, the magick turning me into a conduit, a bolt of lightning.

I'd been riding this last orgasm for what felt like minutes before Gareth and Andrus finished simultaneously and my climax peaked, shattering me apart. When my shuddering ceased, my wolf helped me to my feet. They watched with various emotions streaming through the bond as I approached Felix. Thankfully, he'd taken off the sweatpants.

There was something conflicted in him as he studied my approach. A mix of nerves, cocky assuredness and something else... a warm, fuzzy kind of feeling. But before I could study it further, he distracted me by sweeping me up in his arms and carrying me to the balcony railing. It was just wide enough to sit on without feeling like you'd fall with one wrong move and he placed me there, spreading my thighs wider as he moved close.

But he couldn't shake his tension.

"Are you alright?" I asked Felix.

He cast a sidelong glance at the others. "Sure. It just didn't feel like an audience was watching last time."

I looked over and saw the other three standing, arms crossed, and I sighed.

"Guys, come on. He was honest, you can't fault him for that. I'd prefer he be up-front instead of pretending there's love where there isn't. Some people don't operate that way."

A thrum of acceptance from Gareth and Andrus pulsed through the bond, but from Felix I felt... regret?

Again, before I could look closer, Felix kissed me, running his hands down my back to settle on my ass. I hooked my legs around him and pulled him closer still, trapping his cock between us. I ground against him, sliding along his shaft, working him up.

He chuckled and pushed back against the vise grip of my legs until I relented. He lined up and drove into me. We groaned in unison and the hesitancy disappeared, the magick resuming its swirling, electric hum.

My pussy pulsed frantically as Felix opted for long, deep strokes, dragging against my walls as they tightened around him, driving me wild.

I met every thrust until Felix changed positions, helping me off the railing and turning me around. His tip probed my ass, and he paused.

"Yes," I said, moaning as he pushed into me. I rocked back into him and he gasped as I took all of him without pause, letting the sweet ache roll through me as it turned quickly into pleasure. He braced his hands on either side of mine and eased himself out and in until my tight ring allowed for easier passage, before spurring his pace. I pushed back against him with every thrust, his hips slamming into me. I shifted so I could support myself with one arm crooked on the railing while I slid my other hand between my thighs, gasping as my body tightened with climax so near the surface.

We crashed together one final time as we came and the gardens below us got hazy as my vision clouded. We caught our breath and separated.

When I turned, Remi was there. We stared at each other for a moment as the colors of my eyes mesmerized him.

Moving slowly, like we had all the time in the world, Remi picked me up and carried me back inside. The others sensed they should stay behind as Remi walked us to the smaller bedroom he'd chosen and closed the door. The bed was still plenty big, though.

Still with the same patient slowness, Remi set me on the bed.

CHAPTER FOURTEEN

Remi

"Perfect," I said, as I gazed down at Meg. Her face was flushed and she was so beautiful, matching the person I knew her to be through and through.

I climbed onto the bed and lay beside her, stroking her face. My breath hitched as her eyelashes fluttered over those entrancing eyes, shining in the room's darkness. I was already hers. Had been since I saw her bravery and refusal to give up.

I just hoped she'd have me.

"Can you lay back?" she asked. I nodded and settled back so my growing wings weren't flat on the bed. And then she explored me. With her lips, her fingers. Tracing my scars and placing light kisses on the worst ones. Head to toe, she ventured, and I watched. There was no fear, no disgust at my scarred and damaged body.

She grasped my cock in her hand, her fingers not able to fully close around my girth. Her eyes flicked to me and my breath caught as her tongue slid across the tip, her hand working its way along my shaft. She ducked her head, and my eyes closed at the wonderful feel of her mouth closing around me. She gripped my balls with her other, massaging, and a loud groan worked its way up from my toes.

I forced my eyes open so I could watch her swallow my cock. I gripped her hair as her saliva glistened along my length in the low light. My edge was approaching fast.

"Wait," I choked out.

I needed to have her so badly it was all I could do to pace myself. Not until I'd already tasted her and made her scream my name, would I allow myself to take her completely.

Meg paused and stared into my eyes, teasingly swirling her tongue around me.

We switched positions, and I eagerly moved between her thighs, spreading them wide as I dipped my head to get my first taste. My tongue laved her sensitive nub, and she whimpered. I moved two fingers into her slick warmth and pulsed as I continued my ministrations.

Her back arched off the bed and her fingers wrapped in my hair. My stubble brushed against her thighs as I continued to lick her, fingers pumping.

Her gasps were more frequent, and her pussy fluttered around my fingers. With the flat of my tongue, I pressed against her nub and she came, bucking against my hand.

"Oh, gods! Remi!"

When the spasms around my fingers slowed, I moved back up her body, kissing her softly as I settled between her thighs.

She bared her neck for me, and I growled in approval, my teeth grazing the thin skin. My tongue traced her clavicle, and I placed kisses along her chin before dipping my head back down to lick and nip at her throat. I nuzzled my nose behind her ear, and she moaned loudly, straining against my cock. I moved my mouth to that spot and her breath turned to soft pants, breasts heaving. Fastening my mouth around one of the taut pink buds, I swirled my tongue over her nipple before grazing it with teeth. Her back arched again, pushing toward the pleasure.

I couldn't wait any longer. Grasping her hips, I sank my cock into her. I moved slowly, not wanting to hurt her. I was much larger compared to the others.

Her walls stretched around me as I moved deeper. Meg shifted her position as we went, but her sighs and moans spurred me onward.

Finally, I was fully sheathed. Meg reached up to stroke my jaw and bring me in for a kiss as we waited for her to adjust to me. When she was ready, I rocked into her, starting with small thrusts. The bonding magick was heavy on us and I could tell it was affecting her. Her skin flushed and dampened with sweat, and I got the first inklings that it was taking hold of me as well.

It started as a prickling that swept into a charged tingling, searing across my skin. I moved faster, plunging deeper, and her knees clamped against my hips as her hands slid across my chest.

The magick roiled within me, alighting every nerve ending as our lovemaking reached a peak. There was a burst of energy and a pain in my back followed by a new weight that made me pause.

Meg gasped with surprise. "Your wings," she breathed.

I barely dared to look, but I risked a glance in the mirror on the far wall. There they were. My wings had grown back all at once. Joy overtook me as I looked back at my mate. She gave them back to me, quick and all but painless. I unfurled them to their full span before pulling them back in and held her close, still inside her as I walked us back out to the balcony. The others stared after us in shock, but I paid them no mind.

"Your skin," she said, cupping my cheek.

My skin was building its stoney shield, and I knew she would witness my skin graying and my eyes changing to a clear silver.

"Oh," she breathed, squirming a bit.

"Sorry, should have warned you." The tough stone skin always added a bit of thickness... to everything.

"I'm not complaining," she said with a sly smile, moving herself along my cock. "Are you planning what I think you're planning?"

I kissed her in response, and unfurled my wings, beating them heavily to test them out before I took off into the air. We soared up faster than I intended, and I brought us up short. "Still alright?" I asked a breathless Meg. She looked down at the ground far below us.

"This is amazing."

My hips surged forward in response and she bit her lip, stifling a moan. "Do you trust me?" I asked.

She rested her forehead against mine. "Completely."

I flipped over in the air in a barrel roll and she shrieked, falling against my chest and laughing as I straightened out, catching a current of air and flying on my back, her astride me. Meg rode me, repositioning to better brace herself and set a steady pace.

As we coasted, I slipped into other air currents as we ran into them, turning, rolling, a constant change of position to delay our climax. When we were both desperate for our release, I shifted us once again, wrapping my hands under her thighs. I drove up into her and she cried out, wrapping her legs tighter to gain leverage as she met me.

I dove and rolled, thrusting deeper with each beat of my wings to drive me. The ground was coming up fast, and the bond wrapped around us tight as we neared the finish.

Meg gasped her release, and the bond snapped into place, linking us all together. I came, filling her just as I pulled up and set us gently on the ground.

"Show off," yelled Andrus from the balcony, laughing.

Instead of heading back for the house, Meg led us toward a grotto filled with night-blooming jasmine. She lay on the ground, and I took up a place beside her as we stared up at the stars.

She reached for my hand, and I wrapped my fingers in hers.

The others joined us after a time, and we slept.

When I woke, the sun was just peeking over the walls of the grotto. Meg was curled against my chest, and I was taken again by how beautiful she was. I stroked the hair away from her face and when my fingers brushed her cheek, I felt the smooth hardness of stone.

Her eyes cracked open and focused on me. "Good morning."

I smiled down at her and clasped the hand resting on my chest. It, too, was hard and unyielding, but maintained her normal skin tone.

"I guess we know what power you share with me."

Meg blinked and looked at her hand. She clenched her fingers together and knit her brow. "I don't feel any—"

She put her hand to her cheek and there was the faintest sound of stone clinking against stone.

Her movement had awakened the others. Gareth was on her other side, and as he came awake, he realized something was different.

"Stone skin?" he asked, voice groggy with sleep. "That'll come in handy."

Meg greeted him with a kiss, and Andrus, who had stood to stretch, leaned down for a kiss of his own. Felix was gone.

She was staring at her hand, and I felt the faintest shimmer of magick wash over her. Her skin became soft and pliable again, and when she tapped her fingers together, there was no sound.

Another wash of magick and her skin became stone. "I think I've got it."

We headed for the house, and I caught movement from the balcony. Felix was leaning over the edge, staring at the garden. He'd freshly plaited his hair and looked contemplative. Through the bond, I could feel confusion from someone, and I only needed one guess to know who.

Andrus noticed as well. "He seems to have taken some of what you said to heart."

Meg nodded. "He's conflicted about something. What we're asking of him is contrary to everything he's ever lived by, except for the loyalty he shares with you. I'm kind of the seventh wheel in this scenario."

"Give him a chance," I said. "Once he gets into the fight with the rest of us, he might begin to see things differently."

We entered the house and stole up the back stairs, hoping not to catch the attention of the staff already at work in the kitchen. After an... eventful shower, we headed back down for breakfast, determined to enjoy the day before Death came to call.

Chapter Fifteen

Meg

"A re you ready?" Death held out his hand.

"Why do I get the feeling that when you ask people that question it's usually under different circumstances? This is temporary, right?" I was only half joking.

"My dear, when I pick people up to shuffle them off their mortal coil, I don't ask if they're ready because they never are." He grinned. "Now, are you ready?"

The portal was shimmering just behind him, destination not set. "What's so different about this portal that Hades won't detect it?"

Death *tsked* at me, shaking his finger back and forth. "Those are my secrets. If I went about sharing that information with everyone, people would be popping up all over the place where they were uninvited. That would undoubtedly lead to a spike in deaths, which would ultimately just make my job harder."

"Be careful," said Andrus, wrapping me in his arms. He placed a light kiss on my lips before releasing me. Remi and Felix repeated the gesture, but of course, Gareth was still having none of it.

He'd warned me that this would happen, even apologized in advance for when his alpha personality took over, and his domination got in the way. Even so, I was having a very hard time not losing my patience with him.

"I still don't like this," he said, crossing his arms and planting his feet in a wide stance. "If even one of us was allowed to go with you—"

"We don't have time for your posturing, wolf," said Death, his tone clipped. "She needs to go, and you need to carry out the mission I gave you. There is no debate to be had. Just do it."

"But—"

"You do not want to make an enemy of me," Death snapped. "Keep this up, and you may find that once your mission is complete, this group will be down a man. I am still lord and master of death, and I will wield my power as I see fit. Nobody is immune, deal or not."

Gareth's mouth snapped shut and I crossed the couple of paces to him. "I'll be okay. I know the terrain, I can move quickly. It'll be all right. I'll see you all again soon."

My wolf crushed me to him, pulling back just enough to look into my face. "You better." He kissed me deeply, and I melted into him. Death cleared his throat

"Today, please."

I broke away, Gareth holding my hand, our fingertips brushing as I stepped out of range. I took a deep breath and looked ahead at the portal.

"Let's go."

Death moved me forward until my toes were right at the edge. "You might want to hold your breath."

I shot him a confused glance right before he shoved me through. A yelp escaped my throat as I fell, wind tearing at me, stealing whatever air was left in my lungs. It felt like I was caught in a tornado, hurtling at a breakneck speed, being tossed this way and that. I didn't know up from down.

Dizziness overtook me and I struggled to keep my eyelids closed, tears running down my cheeks.

And then I landed.

Even though I'd called this place home for over fifty years, this landscape didn't look familiar. Maybe I'd done a good job of blocking out the horrid memories I had of being here.

Death said he would set me down as close as he could to where he thought Arthur might be. Assumedly, he would have just as much an ability to sense souls as I did.

As I stood here in this vast, gray emptiness again, I doubted that assertion.

Most of the souls that wound up here would be wandering on the plains of the dead. When I was growing up, I hated going anywhere near that place. It was always so sad. The souls slowly lost their memories, anything that tied them to their old lives. But the ones that were still holding onto hope that they might reunite with some of their loved ones were the hardest to witness.

They would have just enough wherewithal to grieve and ask questions of people who had no answers. They would be stuck in a perpetual cycle of sadness and anguish with no end in sight. It was its own kind of hell, and the harder they clung onto that hope, the longer they would linger in that state. Hundreds of years, just looking for a familiar face that they probably wouldn't recognize anymore, even if they did see it.

Very rarely did any souls wander into this portion of the underworld. The perimeters were the haunts of various creatures, most of them dangerous. Things that were more phantom than animal, with just enough substance to make them hungry. Souls that wandered too close didn't last long, and once they were consumed by the roaming beasts, they would cease to exist entirely, nothing left even for reincarnation.

The good thing was, since I was here in a physical body, most of them wouldn't bother me. But it did make travel much more difficult. Death had made it very clear that if I tried to use any of my power here, I would light up like a damn beacon. So once again, I was left with little choice but to wander until I found something, some clue, to lead me to Arthur.

The landscapes looked different, and I had to focus on finding landmarks I recognized to stay on track. The air was thick and humid. Moisture clung to my skin. The ground was marshy, and my feet were already freezing, the cold water seeping into my shoes. Within the hour, every step had become a slog, like trudging through syrup, or wet sand. My hair stuck to my face, and I pushed the damp strands away, attempting to make a loose braid, but it only tangled. I gave up and let it fall.

There was a soft noise to my right, no louder than you'd expect of a chipmunk stepping on a leaf and scurrying into the underbrush. I looked over and leaped back as a rambling form stepped in front of me, completely oblivious that I was even there. The massive creature had long shaggy hair, kind of like a sloth, complete with moss growth on the strands. Two spiraling horns stretched upward from its head and a long snout filled with flat teeth tilted up as it scented the air, nostrils the diameter of softballs.

Not finding anything of interest, it rambled on, still making almost no noise in its passing.

Something else I'd forgotten since leaving here was the fatigue that would always set in, the underworld leeching out any life force it could find. It took a specific shielding to protect yourself from it, but I didn't dare risk it. The only people who used those shields were the Stranger residents of this realm and they wouldn't be caught dead here, no pun intended.

This was the wild, great unknown. The sophisticated denizens of the underworld never set foot in these places, preferring instead to hole up in their palaces, enjoying the finer things in life while being waited on by their service staff of spirits.

Part of me was curious, in a morbid kind of way, to see my old home again. I knew my keepers were long dead. Bel had made sure of that, and I didn't mourn their loss. But I wondered if I would get some kind of closure for all those miserable years.

I stopped. Just ahead was a giant boulder, cracked down the middle, one-half crumbled into the grass, nothing more than pebbles. I knew that landmark, had seen it many times from the other side, which meant the city was close. And if that was the case, I needed to go east. That's where the plains would be.

The walk was long and arduous. The landscape changed little; scrub, to slightly taller scrub, switching to stunted trees, and then back to scrub. All the beautiful landscape was around the city.

Here it was just as desolate as the souls that wandered it. I saw the first wanderers after what must've been a full day of travel. A small group, none of them acknowledging each other, just traveling in the same direction. They all had equally vacant looks on their faces. I moved past them. Their eyes seemed to focus briefly on me, recognizing me as something other before they slipped past, and all signs of consciousness disappeared.

Their clothing was all in muted shades of gray. As far as I knew, whatever you died in was roughly what you appeared in here, just lacking any color. Skin turned gray, eyes lost their color and became an opaque silver. Hair, too, bleached to white. The only things that ever stood out were bruises or wounds with fresh blood, for those who died a violent death. Their bodies would be whole, but the evidence of the trauma they suffered would be there.

Pretty soon, the number of souls increased, the groups becoming larger, almost like herds. They wandered together because it made sense, a comfortable habit, but they never spoke.

I was moving against the flow of traffic when I noticed a wanderer standing alone, staring around, and muttering to themselves. The spirit lifted a hand to its mouth and chewed on its nails. As I got closer, I noticed it was a young man, in his late teens or early twenties. His clothing would put him roughly from the early 2000s, so compared to the other souls around him, he was a recent arrival.

And he was clearly a soul clinging to memories. I attempted to skirt him, not wanting him to notice and latch on to me. I wasn't trying to be cold or heartless, but there was nothing I could do to help him.

Unfortunately, my attempts to evade him didn't work. Out of the corner of my eye, I saw his head snap in my direction and I cursed under my breath.

"Hey!" he shouted, hurrying toward me. He fell into step beside me. "Can you help me?"

I heaved a sigh. "No, I'm sorry."

He stammered. "But you don't even know what I was going to ask you."

I stopped and turned. "Yes, I do. You were going to ask me to help you find a loved one. Or ask me where you are. Or if I know the way out."

The man's mouth snapped shut and he stared at me, confused.

"I can't help you. You've passed on. This is the realm of the dead. Please believe me, the sooner you forget, the better off you'll be."

"But—"

"Trust me. Once you let yourself go, reincarnation will happen a lot faster for you. You won't be stuck here forever. It's just a holding place. Where you can get ready for the next go-round."

"But—" His face was distraught. "Please, can't you help me?"

I turned and walked away, my quick steps becoming a jog as he screamed after me. "Why won't you help me?"

The plains were a large, open, flat area, as befit the name, so I was in his sights for a long time before he finally quieted. The crush of souls around me was so thick now that I didn't see how I was ever going to find Arthur without using my abilities.

When I couldn't bring myself to take another step, I climbed up an embankment that would be out of the way of the herds and rested. I watched the countless wanderers pass before me, scanning each face briefly, hoping to see the one I was looking for.

I hadn't given a lot of thought to how I was going to approach Arthur when I found him. Butterflies were constant in my stomach. I'd betrayed him, allowed Bel to torture and kill him. And then he'd visited me in my dreams, forgiven me for what I'd done. Even appeared as an apparition after he'd died for one last goodbye.

My thoughts wandered to our original meeting when he revealed he knew who I was. That earnestness, that hope that he'd had, that the waiting was over, and he could finally continue with the mission that he'd been charged with millennia ago.

But then there was Sasha. A pang of guilt tore through me.

I'd seen the way he looked at her, the love he had for her. Despite what transpired between us—that kiss—there was no doubt in my mind that he truly loved her. The overwhelming realizations of that moment when we came face-to-face got the better of both of us. But in a way, I was still a home-wrecker. I'd torn him away from his wife, who had never shown me anything but kindness.

My mates had found other partners in their long period of waiting, of course. But Arthur and Remi were the only ones who had actually gotten married. I guess we didn't know about Hadi yet, but the dynamics of our group were already so complicated. Remi would never be able to lay the memories of his wife and children to rest. So even after I recovered Arthur, would the ghost of Sasha's memory constantly haunt us too?

I was caught in that miasma of conflict when hope reignited.

Chapter Sixteen

Felix

I watched the portal blink closed behind our mate with a sinking feeling. Not necessarily that something would go wrong, but... I couldn't put my finger on it.

Death turned to us. "Here we are. Are you ready for your task?"

"We don't have a choice, so just tell us," growled Remi. I raised my eyebrows, surprised that he spoke to Death that way.

Death shook his finger with a fake stern look. "Always with the attitude." The humor melted away. "I'm going to start giving warnings and if you lot don't heed them... well. What do the kids say? Fuck around and find out?" He sniffed and smoothed out his lapels in a sort of nervous tick.

"When Meg retrieves Arthur's soul, he'll need a body to get back to."

My heart sank. I hadn't even thought about that.

Death continued. "His original body will be the best choice, but if that isn't possible, we'll need to figure out another avenue."

Andrus balked. "He's been gone for at least a month. There's no way his body would be a viable choice."

Death grinned. "That would be the natural assumption. But Belsioch had a nice little pocket dimension that he would send everyone to when he finished torturing them. Arthur died at his hands, but he disposed of the body in that dimension."

"How do you know?" I asked.

His face reminded impassive, and he stared at me, wordless.

"Right. It's your purview," I said.

"But wouldn't it be rotted away?" asked Gareth.

"I expected better from you," Death said to the wolf. He shook his head, sighing with exasperation that he needed to explain all this. "The pocket dimension doesn't function like the normal world. Time works differently. And if I know anything about Belsioch, it's that he'd want to prolong whatever suffering he could. I'm sure he would've put Arthur in there, alive and mortally wounded if he could have. He just got carried away. After he'd inflicted maximum pain, he would toss his victims into their prison, where every day was as long as a life-age of the earth."

Death studied his fingernails. "Arthur should still be fresh as a daisy. Unless a hungry critter got to him first." He clapped his hands together. "Off you get! Bring me back a body to stuff that soul into."

We four shared a look, wondering who was going to ask the question.

"How do we find this pocket dimension?" Andrus ventured.

"Ah, right." Death motioned behind him and a portal appeared. "Oh, and you'll need these." Another flick of the wrist and swords appeared, strapped to our waists. We examined them, and I found mine acceptable. I would've preferred something heavier, but it would do in a pinch.

"Anything else we should—"

"No," said Death, already bored.

What else could we do? The four of us headed through the portal to whatever awaited us.

On the other side of that portal was a nightmare made real.

Thick forest surrounded us, so dense we couldn't move without making a terrible amount of noise. The air stank with the smell of death and the air was hot, humid and still. Water dripped from the leaves. Every time a drop would fall on my head, I'd half expect to find some horrible creature had landed on me.

Small eyes peered at us from the twilight, glinting before moving on. Large spiderlike creatures moved through the underbrush, the shushing noise as they darted through thick growth raising all the hairs on my arms. Croaking noises that sounded like communication between the beasts tracked us as we moved.

Gareth had taken the lead, his time in the dense forests of ancient Briton giving him more experience with this terrain than the rest of us.

Growls followed us, but the movements of the creature made almost no noise. If it didn't give itself away by growling, we wouldn't even know it was—

A shape leaped at my face from the opposite direction the growl had come from. I slashed with my sword and sliced it cleanly in half.

"What the hell is that thing?" I asked, wiping its blood off my face. It stank like nothing I'd ever smelled before, and I could feel it burning me where it made contact.

The creature itself was long and sinuous, but it had legs and a ridge of sharp, jagged bone jutting from its spine.

Andrus shook his head. "No idea."

Remi had changed his skin to stone, the lucky bastard.

"I don't suppose you could fly up and try to find him from overhead?" I asked, but a brief glance at the tightly woven canopy told me everything I needed to know.

"Even if I got through the trees, unless he's in a clearing..." I nodded.

"But maybe I could take a look just to see what's around. Give us some idea of where to go?"

"Worth a shot," said Andrus.

Remi's wings couldn't even get clearance in this thicket, so he climbed a tree until he found enough space to maneuver. He punched through the canopy and disappeared.

After that initial attempted strike by the lizard-thing, there wasn't much else of note. The light never changed, and we continued to trek. Every once in a while we'd hear Remi's wings fly overhead as he searched. At least, I hoped it was him.

He circled around again and yelled at us. "Call out!"

"Here!" bellowed Gareth. Leaves and branches fell on us as Remi crashed through, snagging on a branch. He cursed. "This place is impenetrable. How are we supposed to find a body? Even if we could track signatures like Meg can, he's dead. There wouldn't be one."

"I guess it doesn't really matter that much. No time will pass in the outside world, right? Plenty of time to find him before Meg gets back with his soul," said Andrus. Even he was struggling to put a positive spin on this place.

"What if we try to find the doorway?" asked Gareth. "Belsioch has to have a regular point of entry, right? And if Arthur was already dead, I doubted he carried him deep into the forest to hide him somewhere."

"Good idea," I said. "Who knows how to track gates?"

"I do," said Remi.

"Since when?" I asked, having expected one of the other two to answer.

He shrugged. "Since today, I guess. It's the strangest thing. There's a haze at the corners of my vision. When I let my focus go slack, it's like another world overlays on this one. Can Meg do that?"

"It might be similar to how she tracks signatures," said Andrus. "What do you see here?"

Remi stared around him. As he turned behind us, he leaped back with a shout, drawing his sword.

"What is it?" snapped Gareth.

There was silence, Remi staring into the gloom.

"Remi?" he tried again.

"It's just staring at me," Remi said. "It's massive."

"I don't see anything," I said, looking at Andrus. "Do you?"

An ear-piercing shriek broke the silence and trees toppled as a gigantic shape pushed into view. Its body was green, blending with the surrounding foliage. It had too many limbs, none of them the same size, and more than a dozen eyes. It lunged, moving with an unnerving gait. Its flesh undulated and as I looked closer—I gagged, nausea threatening to spill my lunch.

Millions of parasites crawled over it, over each other, sharp legs leaving punctures in the other parasites, from which squeezed more of the things.

Another shriek allowed us to see the several rows of bloody, broken teeth in its gaping maw.

"Run!" shouted Remi.

We didn't ask follow-up questions, pelting through the undergrowth. Tree limbs slashed my face as I pushed through the foliage. The beast wasn't giving up. A wave of parasites detached from it and gave chase. We'd be overrun. I tapped into my magick and wrapped us each in a concealment cloak. The monsters paused in their pursuit, but they could still hear us. I added echoes, twisting the sounds until we were surrounded by a wall of crashing noise.

That finally stopped them in their tracks, and as the enormous beast caught up to them, it howled with rage. We kept running until even the faint echoes of its roars faded.

We stopped to catch our breaths. "Remi, you need to find that doorway. We have to get out of here," I said, leaning on my knees as I gasped for breath. Gods, I was out of shape.

"Give me a minute," he said, not much better off than me.

"How many more things like that do you think are running around out here?" asked Gareth. He wasn't even winded.

Andrus glared at him. "Why would you ask that? Are you trying to jinx us?"

Gareth shrugged. "It was just a question."

"A horrifying question," said Andrus.

"Wait. I think I see something," said Remi. "North of here. There's some kind of distortion that looks different from everything else."

"How far?" I asked, still bent over double. "Asking for a friend."

Remi smirked. "Far."

"Fuck," I huffed.

"Let's move," said Gareth. "If you think your *friend* is capable of it."

"He's perfectly well, thank you. And he also told me to tell you this," I said, making a rude hand gesture as I straightened.

Gareth grinned and motioned for Remi to take the lead. "Can you twist another illusion around us? Hide us and block our sound from getting out?"

I shot him a look. "You know I can. It's going to get loud, though. We'll have to stop a lot."

So we continued with our journey, stuck in an echo chamber where the sound redoubled with every step until the noise became so deafening we had to stop, stay still until the noise faded, and then carry on.

But it beat having to come face-to-face with a monster like that again.

As we passed unnoticed through the forest, we saw a great many more creatures lounging casually, or eating, or fighting and then eating the loser. None of them made sense by the standards of what we were familiar with, which was a lot. Did Belsioch dream this shit up himself, or did he discover this place?

"Wait," said Remi. "We're close. Keep a lookout."

Now that we were coming to it, I was afraid to look too close. Even if we were planning on restoring Arthur to his body, it didn't make it easier to think about finding his corpse.

It soon became clear that this was indeed a dumping ground for Belsioch's victims. Corpses were strewn everywhere.

More than once, I tripped over one that had crawled to find a place to hide before they died.

Each one was mangled, and it was impossible to tell if it was a monster or Belsioch's doing, although I guess those terms weren't mutually exclusive.

I didn't know if I could handle seeing my oldest friend like this.

Arthur wasn't fae, but he'd grown up in fae lands. He was switched with a changeling as a child, but the faeries that stole him for a pet tired of him and turned him out on his own. He survived in the wilds of faeryland until a hunting trip brought me into his line of sight. We wanted the same stag, and he almost shot me for it, his crude bow still accurate enough to be deadly.

What started as attempted murder became a fast friendship, and I convinced him to come to the court with me, to beg the queen for residency. There were trials she made him pass, of course, but she allowed me to stay with him and see him through.

"Over here! I found him!" yelled Andrus.

The others raced over to him, but I couldn't make myself move fast. I readied myself for what I knew I was about to see.

The grim looks on my brother's faces confirmed it. Remi wiped a hand down his face and turned away. Gareth kneeled next to him but couldn't look at the body.

As I approached, the sickness that threatened my stomach earlier succeeded. I grabbed onto a tree and vomited, the sour taste filling my mouth and nose. Wiping my mouth on the back of my hand, I took a steadying breath and approached.

He was ruined. There wasn't an inch of skin that wasn't cut, bruised, stabbed, or torn. Healing bruises were everywhere, so he'd suffered for a long time before Belsioch put him out of his misery. An anguished moan sounded, and I realized it had come from me.

Remi clapped a steadying hand on my shoulder. "Let's get him out of here."

Gareth and Andrus nodded and lifted Arthur. Death had been right. He looked like he'd only just died. Some of the blood still looked fresh.

"Will Death know when we got the body?" Remi asked.

We looked at each other, stomachs sinking. How were we supposed to get back?

"Um," said Andrus, but he stopped.

The outline of a doorway had appeared in midair and we breathed a sigh of relief. It opened, and we rushed through, eager to leave this place behind. It wasn't until the doorway closed behind us that we realized something was wrong.

We were in basement, full of technology I wasn't familiar with, but I knew it was farther in the future than the '80s. A wall was full of shelves lined with cataloged objects, some of which I recognized.

"Where are we?" I asked.

"Vermont," said a cheerful female voice. We turned and saw a tall woman standing by a desk. Nephilim, unless I missed my guess.

"Who are you?" asked Remi.

"My name is Risha," she said. "We need to talk."

Chapter Seventeen

Meg

I t started as a gentle tug at the back of my thoughts, a subtle presence that pulled my attention to the south. It was the direction I had been traveling, but now I had full confidence that I would find my quarry. I hopped down from the embankment and continued on, moving swift and sure, against the tide.

The sea of faces became a blur. At the end of the next day, the sensations were palpable. I could feel Arthur's presence like a heat, pulsing ahead of me. Drawing me in. I picked up my pace, first a jog and then a run. He was right ahead of me now. Had to be.

There was a large group ahead, and I ran at them full tilt. "Arthur!"

There he was, toward the middle, staring straight ahead with the same blank look on his face as all the others. I pushed my way through the crowd, stopping in front of him, but he sidestepped and kept walking, not even sparing me a glance.

"Arthur, wait!" I reached out and grabbed his arm. He stopped, but didn't turn to face me. He stood stock-still as I circled around to look him in the eye. He was much taller than me, same as the others, and I peered upward, searching. His gaze never wavered. He kept staring resolutely forward, and even when I put myself in his line of sight, his stare blasted right through me.

I put my hands on his face, stroking his cheeks with my thumbs. "Arthur?"

He took a step forward, pushing past me and almost knocking me down. I grabbed his arm again, he stopped, and we repeated the same process.

Nothing I did or said got through to him. Death had been pretty vague on what the other "workarounds" were, but he seemed to be confident. Although the more I got to know him, the more it appeared that he was *always* confident.

I didn't have much of a choice. We had to leave. I couldn't waste any more time. Every extra second I spent here was another opportunity for Hades to realize what was happening.

With my palm firmly planted in the middle of Arthur's chest to prevent him from walking off, I called forth the portal. The instant it opened, it felt like I was caught in a scene from the Lord of the Rings, as Sauron's eye fixed on our location.

Much too slow for comfort, I watched the portal open with agonizing tension, feeling like a million eyes were watching us. "Come on, come on," I said, motioning my hand in the universal signal for *hurry the fuck up.*

The gate stretched open, and I pushed Arthur toward it, his every movement fighting me like I was trying to move a robot. At that same moment, I felt a presence behind me and the edges of the gateway started to shrink. Horrified, I shoved Arthur through, carrying myself with him by sheer momentum.

Time seemed to slow, and not of my doing. Arthur tipped through and fell as a hand closed around my arm and yanked me back, the doorway snapping shut with me still stuck in the underworld.

I stared, dumbfounded, at the blank space where the portal had been. The grip tightened, and I turned. Long, slender hands with sharp black nails and fingertips. Like they'd dipped their fingers in a pot of ink, held them up and let it drip down to coat their skin.

My eyes traveled up the arm, pale, exposed skin like alabaster covering a wiry, but strong shoulder. Straight black hair fell in a curtain around a delicately pointed face. Enormous eyes with vibrant, purple irises, hauntingly similar to my own, stared back at me.

The grin twisting her mouth took the breath from my lungs. Her lips were so red and glossy it was almost grotesque, because they weren't painted with any kind of lip stain. It reminded me of raw meat and flayed muscle. They contorted around perfect teeth in the semblance of a smile, but it was cold. Dead.

Her cheeks had two perfect circles of blush, and her ears rose into absurd points that jutted away from her head. She had to be one of the most bizarre creatures I'd ever seen.

This woman twitched as she stood, her grip unmoving, reminding me of a marionette getting its strings readjusted. And when she spoke, it was even worse.

"Master Hades requests your presence."

The voice didn't match the creature. It was gravelly and hard, full of bass that rumbled out of her chest. The best thing

I could compare it to would be a broken voice box in a vintage toy, the ones where you pull the cord and wait for it to talk. Her mouth opened, but her lips never moved, and I noticed only the stump of a tongue.

"How could I turn down that invitation?" I asked, kind of hoping she'd answer me literally. No such luck.

"Follow me," she said, turning and walking stiffly. I had no choice but to follow. I'm sure the alternative was getting chased down by Cerberus.

Even by my standards, time flowed very strangely in the underworld. Sometimes it seemed we were traveling for days and making no progress. Other times, the surrounding landscape would change so drastically in what felt like minutes that it left my head spinning.

Pretty soon, the desolate landscape gave way to lush gardens, greenswards, villas dotting a countryside greener than a pasture in Ireland. Artificial sunlight was streaming from overhead. We'd reached civilization.

This area was divided up into circles, concentrically nestled inside each other. It was all arranged around a hill, atop which stood Hades's house. The Gieses had lived in a circle just outside of Hades's palace. I had never met him directly. My keepers trotted me out to one of his parties more than once, but rarely did he even attend them. He would make a brief appearance, just for the sake of being a host, and disappear.

When we reached the first gate in the outer circle, none of the guards even looked at us. The walls were mostly for show. Occasionally, you might have a great hero on his hero's journey busting in and trying to steal something, or break somebody out. And of course, that one time, when Bel had swept in, murdered my keepers and everybody else in the house, stolen me away, and left it burning.

But those were very rare.

It was exactly the same as I remembered it, even fifty years later. Bright white pea gravel lined the streets. Everybody here traveled on foot, the only vehicles being the occasional palanquin, carried by long-dead servants. The houses on this level were modest, mostly single-story. Brightly colored stucco covered in murals immediately drew the eye, putting the visitor at ease. Once you reached this city, it was far from the doom and gloom you might expect in the land of the dead.

The gate to the next circle was only a few hundred yards away, the main road here leading straight up to the palace. Each circle had a single row of houses lining either side, with markets present in each. Only a few hundred people actually *lived* here. The others were dead, either indentured ghosts that ran the homes, or reanimated bodies that did things like farm or carry litters.

Any of the living that we passed didn't recognize me. Or if they did, they didn't acknowledge me. I've never been out unless I was in somebody's charge, and usually concealed under a veil or in my own palanquin, completely enclosed, and curtains shut tight. It was less out of a desire to protect me from being discovered, than it was to treat me as their secret weapon. If I was seen too often, the allure would be gone.

The next circle had the same set up, just with slightly larger houses. And so it went, stucco giving away to marble, which gave away to gold and silver. Things got gradually more extravagant until the opulence was thick enough to choke on. As we entered the circle where I'd grown up, I noticed the blackened husk of the house still stood, an empty skeleton made of charcoal. Why hadn't they cleared the debris away? Real estate was pretty prime up here.

We stood before the gate to the final circle, and this time we were regarded keenly, but when the guards noticed the servitor that was leading the way, they quickly opened the gate and made themselves scarce until we had passed.

I could feel their eyes boring into us, no small amount of fear emanating from them, and I was pretty sure it was directed at this creature dragging me up the front steps into the house of Hades. That kind of fear was the fear of potential. This marionette had been a person once and had been changed into this horrifying semblance of one.

The palace before us was covered in gleaming pearl, shining with rainbow hues in the sunlight. Clouds shifted overhead and the sun hit the walls with full force, creating a dazzling effect that made me shield my eyes. Light radiated in sweeps and arcs in a blinding display.

We were halfway up the stairs when the massive doors at the top of the wide steps swung open. A man appeared, black shadow billowing around him, tendrils of inky darkness constantly moving, searching for anything to latch onto.

When he saw us, the shadows dispersed to reveal a man in casual black slacks and a t-shirt that fitted to his form perfectly. The outline of his well-muscled shoulders and arms was plainly visible, as was the washboard of his stomach.

Hades didn't skip ab day.

His deeply-toned olive skin was flawless, as befitted a god, and his thin lips grinned widely as he opened his arms in welcome, perfect teeth shining as bright as the palace behind him. Blue highlights shimmered in his black hair as he swept a loose strand from his face.

As we reached the top of the stairs, he gave a small bow at the waist. "Welcome, Megiste. It's been, what? Fifty years?" His eyes hardened and his voice dropped low as he motioned to the remnants of my keeper's manor just visible from here. "Since that nasty business."

I swept into a bow. "Yes, Lord Hades. It's an honor to be in your presence."

He tipped his head back and laughed, and I watched the taut planes of his throat. When he lowered his face to mine, his eyes, formerly black, gleamed with a reddish-brown hue.

"You lie so well."

He turned and swept back into the palace, his puppet gripping my arm and dragging me along behind. The inside of the palace was vast and empty, the walls a more muted gray with marble floors and a golden ceiling. Statues, art pieces, paintings, sticks of dainty furniture dotted the expanse. But it did nothing to lessen the emptiness. This was very reminiscent of the underworld itself. A few lovely things to catch the eye, amid an absolute wasteland.

The servitor led us to a parlor, set off the main hall. It resembled a dainty tea room, with floral patterns, fine china teacups, and server sets rimmed with gold. Elaborate drapes hung from sconces and filtered the sunlight. So far, this was the only room I've seen with signs of pleasant comfort.

"It's my wife's," said Hades, answering my unspoken thoughts. "Says it brings her joy, so why not? And it's a far less intimidating meeting space from where I would normally bring unexpected guests." He motioned to the velvet-upholstered couch, done in a tasteful burgundy wine color, and took a seat himself in a large chair in the same fashion, crossing an ankle over his knee.

The dangerous glint in his eye was still there, but the reddish hue had faded. After so many years of my life spent here, how did I not know more about the king of this realm? I basically grew up down the street, and I was clueless beyond the very basic accords my keepers taught me. The manners I must uphold in underworld company.

I took a seat, smoothing out my skirt in a vain attempt to resist fidgeting. "Why the restraint?" I asked. "I didn't think I would ever be welcome back here after what happened."

"I didn't say you were welcome. I simply haven't decided what to do with you."

"Could I persuade you to let me leave? I have some pretty big things on my agenda coming up. I can't be late. If I'm understanding correctly, there will be dire consequences."

He shook his head. "You have nothing to offer that could sway me in that direction, no."

I wondered if he knew of my allegiance with Death. Or what he would do if he found out? Death had only hinted and how badly their relationship had gone south, but that's where he left it. But if it was bad enough that he didn't feel he could intervene here without serious consequences, the amount of danger I was in right now was in contrast to the surroundings I found myself in.

"So what are we doing here then?" I asked. "Where does this conversation lead us?"

He shrugged casually, not a care in the world. "That's entirely up to you."

I raised my eyebrows. "How so?"

"I suppose by now you've heard word that I have... weakened. Mentally." He laughed, motioning at himself. "Certainly not physically."

I hedged, pretending to watch out the window as I appraised him out at the corner of my eye. "I might've heard something."

A shadow flickered across his face, but quickly dissipated. "I can assure you it's ridiculous."

I inclined my head. "I never thought otherwise."

"There may be some truth to the matter, that the Ætherim are losing their touch overall. But implying a disconnection, a lessening. It's patently untrue. And to say these things about us, I can only imagine how the Titans are doing right now. Living the last several thousand years in complete isolation." He smiled. "Did you get a good look at how dear Belsioch is treating them? The various tortures he's devised." Hades casually flipped his hand. "And that dungeon ghoul of his. What's his name?"

"I don't know. I didn't have the pleasure of making his acquaintance. He was out of the office, thankfully."

Hades threw back his head and laughed again, before offering another of his thousand-watt smiles. "Say you do this thing. You break the Titans free. I remember your family—"

"They weren't my family. They were keepers. Sociopaths, really."

He shrugged. "Whatever they were. They seemed awfully convinced that there would be great reward waiting for them for the job they were doing for the Titans."

I nodded. "They were under that impression. I'm not sure of the truth of it. They never filled me in on specific details. And I didn't ask." I watched him, curious. "Why? Are you interested in collecting on the debt?"

He spread his hands. "I'm merely seeking opportunities. Not for enrichment as much as... a bolstering."

"How so?"

"I don't want to see the Ætherim fade into nothing. Everything decays. I, of all people, know that. I'm surrounded by the evidence of it every day." He scowled. "Whether I will it or not. Our diminishing has been torturously slow."

"So you want them to extend your lives. In better health, or whatever it is you technically live off of."

"No." He shook his head, regretful. "I would like to hasten our end."

Coming Soon

The Primordial Embers Series Continues...
Look for a new release EVERY MONTH, six novellas in total!
Look for Book 5 in the series October 29th, 2024

The Death's Left Hand Series:
Death's Left Hand Book 3 – October 8th, 2024
Death's Left Hand Book 4 – November 12th, 2024

Visit gwydionroyce.com or follow @gwydionroyce on instagram and facebook for the latest updates!